SHINING THROUGH:
BATTLES IN THE PACIFIC

DONOVAN CORZO

EDITED BY Lila Waterfield

Corzo Creations, LLC

"Shining Through"

Dedicated to the love of my life, Kam.

Many thanks to the Tuesday night crowd for letting me bend your ears.

To Shari, who gave me that pen and told me to go and write that novel. I did, and here it is.

To "The Book Rack staff," thanks for letting me hang out for inspiration and research.

To all my family and friends. Thanks for believing in me and for reading the many rough drafts.

To Karl, my friend for over 30 years and my unofficial editor. I appreciate your honesty and experience.

Donovan Corzo

Other Titles by the Author

Traveller Role-Playing Game Supplements:

100 Plots ISBN: E-Book: 978-1-958297-04-9

100 Rendezvous ISBN: E-Book: 978-1-958297-07-0

100 Alien Rendezvous ISBN: (in development)

100 Alien Plots ISBN: (in development)

100 Underworld Rendezvous ISBN: 978-1-958297-10-0

Novels Set in World War Two:

A Time to Shine E-Book ISBN: 978-1-958297-00-1

A Time to Shine Paperback: ISBN: 978-1-958297-01-8

A Time to Shine Hardcover: ISBN: 978-1-958297-02-5

A Time to Shine Audiobook: ISBN: 978-1-958297-03-2

Shine On: Invasion USA: E-Book ISBN: 978-1-958297-06-3

Forthcoming Novels set in WW2

Up in the Clouds (Proposed release August 20, 2023)

Peace Reigns Through

The Wars End

Novels Set Before and during WW2

Tales from Lake Tillery E-Book ISBN: 978-1-958297-56-8-September 11, 2023 projected release

Shining Through Battles in The Pacific

Table of Contents

Foreword 1

Missing September 1943, Pearl Harbor 2

The Beach 4

Another Lifetime Ago 9

Flintknapping 13

Taking Out the Rising Sun 16

Pearl Harbor: October 15th, 1943 Memorial Service for Battle of Bokak Atoll 22

Gwen 39

The Rescue 49

Charleston, South Carolina November 1st, 1943 56

The Nightmares 63

Home to Roost November 15th, 1943 68

Combat & Tactics Training 82

Enigma 92

Sumire 103

Thanksgiving Day, 1943 111

Bibliography: 116

Up in The Clouds 117

Foreword

I have done ample research and will provide a bibliography of sources. I have used basic manuals from the time and believe in giving credit where it is due. Through firsthand accounts, talking with veterans from the times, and listening to their tales, some were gripping, and others were solemn. Not every character you hear about is real; some are amalgamations of several different ones.

I have attempted to follow history closely and stay true to form, but my days may be slightly off. I have also tried to follow the military protocols and expectations. I have taken liberties with some subject matter because the protagonists would still be in college or training until the war is over if I didn't. I am sure others are better than me and could quote minutiae on what I got wrong ad infinitum. To those people, I say, "Get a life and write your novel. It's a work of fiction."

I hope you enjoy reading this and subsequent novels in the series or set in the same period.

Note: This novel uses period dialogue, including racial slurs. They are spoken between persons, in films, on the radio, and written in mass media. Remembering history is critical if we strive to create a better future, and glossing over these details would be a disservice to everyone who fought and died for this better future to be possible.

Missing
September 1943, Pearl Harbor

Nimitz received the news that PC-234 was struck by a torpedo and lost with all hands. The flotilla had fought the enemy for several hours, knocked out two destroyers and one submarine, plus downed over thirty enemy planes. They had done their job well by pulling at least one task force off the objective but had suffered heavy losses with a fifty percent casualty rate. He looked at the list and felt regret, but he knew Daniel wasn't gone. He was missing. He placed the documents in his drawer and locked them. Then he went to his car and told the driver to go to the hospital. He knew Kim-Yee would get off soon and wanted to tell Daniels's wife. They arrived, and he exited and sat on the bench close to the main entrance. He hung his head as he struggled with what to say. He heard her approach, and her face turned white as she saw him slumped on the bench. He rose, and she shook her head; her voice cracked, "No! No!"

He strode towards her, and she staggered, screaming into his shoulder with a wail of anguish. He hugged her and said, "His ship went down, and they are listed as missing. Our boy's not dead. Just unaccounted for. A lot is happening; it could be weeks before everything gets sorted out. If you get any mail from the Navy that is in a manila envelope, don't open it. I will let you know when I know more, "he said as he steered her to the car. Ten minutes later, he dropped her off at her home. He was stone-faced as the car drove away.

"Thank you," she said, her voice barely a whisper. She dabbed her eyes with a kerchief and turned around to see her older sister Miranda and her thirteen-year-old daughter Hailey standing there. Both were barely holding back tears. She walked up the steps and collapsed into the wicker furniture. Miranda came forward, holding the dreaded envelope. Kim-Yee tiredly reached up and took it from her, tore it in half, and then threw it over her shoulder with disdain. Miranda didn't understand as she had already read the letter. "He's not dead. Just missing!" Hailey started crying and threw herself into her mother's arms. She held her tight and stroked her hair, rocking her back and forth. Making shushing noises, 'There, there, Hailey.'

"Daddy's not coming back, is he?"

"No, my love. He's coming back, just not right away. There was a large battle in the Pacific, and your dad oversaw another group at Bokak Atoll. They did their jobs well but suffered a lot of damage. He should return next month."

"You promise?" she asked expectantly.

"I promise. Now get off to bed, but brush your teeth first."

She groaned and walked off, acting like a martyr.

Miranda gave Kim-Yee a sharp look. "Why do you lie?"

"I didn't."

"But the letter said ...."

"I don't care what it said if you couldn't tell," she motioned to the pieces of the letter blowing lazily across the lawn.

"How could you do that?

She rose, went to the kitchen, and reached for the bottle of whiskey. She cracked it open, pulled a coffee cup off the cupboard, filled it with two ounces, opened the fridge, pulled out a Coca-Cola, and popped the top with the opener on the side. She angrily poured it into the cup and lifted it to the sky. "Here's to you, my darling. Come home to me!" then she drank the contents, weeping.

Miranda asked," Why do you cry if he's not dead?"

"Because I miss him."

The Beach

Daniel awoke feeling weightless. His body ached, and he could feel the warm water and the taste of salt and blood hitting his mouth. A wave rolled him over, and he was choking on seawater. He opened his eyes and felt the sand under him. Both hands had reflexively shot out, and he tried to get to his feet but couldn't seem to complete the motion. His ears were ringing, and he could feel the sun beating down. He staggered to the left, and his foot hit something. He knelt in the surf and blearily tried to make out the features. But his eyes couldn't seem to focus. So, he felt around and determined that it was a body, and the man was long dead. He got himself into a position to do a fireman's drag on the corpse when he felt it tug back, and he fell into the surf. He then realized that this was a pilot still wearing his parachute. He undid the buckles and felt around for the knife at the shoulder. He used that to cut away at the risers, and he could free the body from the shroud. He also heard a large plop into the ocean, and his hand reflexively plunged under the water and came up with a pistol. But it was a break loader and not one he was familiar with. That's when it occurred to him that the pilot was Japanese.

He heard murmuring and saw two figures coming toward him. Then they were upon him, steadying him. There was a light slap across his cheek and an air of concern. His ears popped, and the water started draining from them. His eyes focused better, and he saw that it was his executive officer Waisner and other ranks. He quit struggling with the body, and they each grabbed an arm and carried him off the beach to some shade nearby. He blacked out.

Sometime later, he awoke to the smell of a campfire and roasting fish. He was still groggy, and his throat was parched. "Water?" he rasped. A hand gently went behind his head and helped him forward. The liquid that hit his dry, sore throat was coconut milk. He greedily swallowed it until it was pulled away.

"That's enough. Don't want you to have too much and then throw it up," said Waisner.

He opened his eyes and saw that it was night; the stars were very bright, and Waisner's silhouette was bathed in a soft amber glow. He reached up and felt a rudimentary bandage, wincing as he felt a sharp pain. His head was swimming. Waisner was right. He did feel like he would throw up, but the smell of fish made his mouth water. He motioned to the fish, and a leaf was placed in his hand. It contained a piece of fish and a white disk. He mechanically fed himself while trying not to swoon too much. The flesh was warm and soft. The disk crunched, and he tasted rice. "Where?" he asked, and Waisner replied, "From the pilot. He had a tin of these rice disks. Those must have been his emergency rations. We also got a medkit, some flares, and a pistol; he had a map and a codebook on him. Plus, this." he showed him a rising sun scarf and a picture of the pilot and his wife.

"Leave those with the body and make sure he's given a proper burial."

"But sir," another voice started to say, but Daniel cut him off, "He was a fellow warrior. True, our enemy. But he deserves our respect as he fought well and has provided us with these survival items, including part of this meal. See to it."

"Yes, sir," said the voice, and several figures moved away from the fire to follow his orders.

"Sit, rep," he said.

"Well, sir," Waisner replied," Over sixty of us in various states of injury. We don't know how the battle went, but we saw them duking it out for several hours. What hit us? I don't know. But here we are at Bokak Atoll, I think."

"How are we fixed for defenses?"

"Just the pistol, flares, and a few knives. We've got some spears for fishing, and we've put up a rudimentary shelter, but that's just a lean too."

"See to something more permanent for the injured. Tomorrow, assemble some work parties, make some weapons, and have those injured who have use of their hands start weaving grass mats. Send five men to get more coconuts and any other fruit available. Send another party to find potable water and let them refill the empty coconuts with water. See if there are any reeds or cattails in the area, as those top stalks can be roasted and taste like cornbread."

"Really?"

"Yep."

"How do you know that?"

"It was in the Boy Scout Handbook."

"Where?"

"In the Wilderness Survival Section."

"Good to know."

"Did you get a merit badge in it?'

"No. I never even went to camp. My parents thought it was too extravagant an expense."

"Ouch, to be a Scout and not be able to go to camp."

"Waisner, is having a fire a good move? Won't the Japs see the smoke?"

"That's an excellent question, skipper, but how this one was built is genius. The fire is so intense that there is almost no smoke."

"What? Show me."

He was helped to his feet, and they eased their way to the fire. He saw it had been built next to a large rock that kept the glow from being seen. He observed that there were two holes in the ground and the fire was submerged in the first hole, and the air flowed into the second, which fed the fire a lot of oxygen. This caused the fire to burn higher and brighter and released almost no smoke.

"This is called a Dakota Fire Hole."

"Remarkable"

"I'm surprised you didn't know about this one skipper since you seem to always know just about everything. Why is that?"

"Oh, that's easy. Growing up, I was the fat kid no one wanted to play with."

"Pshaw."

"I'm serious. Growing up, I was the Greek kid who brought the weird food to school."

"Like what?"

"Moussaka."

"What's that?"

"An eggplant casserole."

"Oh, that. Seems odd to choose something like a hot dish."

"Well, then there were the Dolmadakia."

He saw the blank look on Waisner's face and said," The rice-stuffed grape leaves."

Waisner asked, "You mean dolmades?"

"Yes. Kids can be cruel. Even the teachers. Of course, they didn't mean to."

"What did they do?"

"They changed my name."

"Why?"

"Well, my actual name of record is Darian Christos Core. But they already had a student enrolled named Dorian. So, they just called me Daniel."

"Wow."

"I'm turning in."

"Yes, sir. Good night."

Daniel awoke sometime later, hearing the gentle breeze and the swaying of the palm trees. That's when he noticed a pinching feeling on his legs. He discovered that he was covered in hermit crabs, and they were using their pincers to try and grab some flesh. He scrambled awake and started pulling them off of him. He smashed them ferociously with a rock one by one until they were dead. He stopped. He was ashamed of himself. He carefully looked around the camp, but everyone was sleeping. He could hear a guard patrolling, but that was it. Then he gathered the remains and placed them into a makeshift cookpot made from a discarded 3" shell casing.

He was able to find a citronella plant, crush the leaves enough to get the oil and smear it all over his exposed skin. Then he went back to sleep, hoping it would ward off the crabs, the mosquitos, and other parasitic insects.

Another Lifetime Ago

Daniel was dreaming about his time on Liberty in Mobile, Alabama. He and some shipmates had three weeks' leave coming to them, and Bill had an uncle who was running a hotel that needed repairs. They got together and decided to pay Uncle Randal a visit as a work party. The agreement was that they would spend one week sprucing up the hotel and could stay for free—a good arrangement.

They got there, and all the supplies were lined up—wood, saws, tarps, kegs of nails, spackling, and paint. Uncle Randal had the idea that the flooring needed to be done first. Then, the railings needed to be assembled, painted, and installed. Some fans also needed to be mounted in the rooms in the corner so that the airflow would be better if the windows were opened. New screens had to be made. They started in the rear and could see that these units needed the most work. The flooring was the most challenging part because they had to remove all the furniture from the back lot and rip out the hardwood. They used crowbars and hammers to get it all up. Then, the area had to be swept. All loose nails were trimmed off; the entire area was cleaned and dried with a Japan dryer to seal out any moisture that might get under the wood and rot it. The demolition took a whole day. Daniel was not very good with a hammer, so he made himself busy sanding down the roughest parts of the furniture and giving them a good coat of varnish. By the end of the day, all the furniture looks relatively newer. Steve McCaskill, a small Irish man with black hair, freckles, and ghost-white skin, busied himself with the fan installations while Chris worked on the next set of rooms, repairing the spackling.

The following day, they laid the wood down and cut the linoleum, a green tiled pattern. Then, the molding was nailed in place, and the final trim work was done. They moved the furniture and bedding back inside, replacing all the mattresses. They made up the beds with hospital corners and moved on to the next set of rooms. Rinse and repeat.

Rust coloring was running down the walls, so they decided against fighting it and had the paint tinted to match. This gave a warm and inviting glow to the rooms. They got some acid and used it to smarten up the ceramic tiles, bathtub, and toilets. They looked brand new when they were done with four units. It took seven days to complete the entire project, but they did it and were very proud of themselves. Uncle Randal was so appreciative that we bought them a case of beer. They were sitting out by the pool with beers in a washtub of ice when a group of girls came by. Joe gave a wolf whistle, and the blonde turned around and said, "Thanks, boys," waving at them good-naturedly.

They noticed that the girls were checking in and decided now would be an excellent time to get cleaned up and make themselves presentable. An hour later, they were back by the pool, and the girls came around giggling. They introduced themselves, and beers were handed around. The girls were students at the local college here for Spring Break and were looking for a good time. Bill said, "I know of a few good places, but what are you gals looking for?"

Terry, the blonde, said, "Oh, you know. The usual, a place where there is dancing and maybe a little singing.

"What's your budget?"

"Well, why ever would you ask such a question?" she said in mock hurt tones.

"Because we can do that right here.", he said as he pulled out a portable radio and turned the music on. He grabbed her by the hand, and they danced a jig around the pool.

Steven found a newspaper and noted that the Sanger Theater downtown might be a suitable place to start. Bill told them the history of the theater as they boarded the bus. Saying, "The Sanger took over a year to construct in 1927 and cost a whopping $500,000, but you can see where they spent all the money as it has three color auditorium lighting, a large organ, and full stage facilities. I've seen some rather large road shows there. The front entrance is grand, with ornamental Greek Statues of Poseidon and Dionysus. Not to mention that the curtains are made of crushed red velvet, and the seats match and are very comfortable."

"Wow, Bill. You know a lot about this place."

"Yeah, well, I grew up here, so I know a thing or two."

"Excellent, so what's on the agenda for tonight."

Steve looked at the paper and said, "It's a vaudeville show."

Kristin, a chubby redhead, said, "We could do worse. We are here to see the sights and have a good time."

"So, vaudeville it is then.", Bill said excitedly.

They saw the show, and it was okay. Kristen remarked, "I liked the juggler. I've never seen someone who could juggle a basketball, an egg, and an apple, then eat the apple and not break the egg."

Then they went to a bar for drinks, and he noticed Kristen was busy guarding the purses. So, he went over to her in a conspiratorial tone and said, "What are you doing?"

"Guarding the purses for the girls."

"Why? Did you lose a bet?"

"Nope. But it's just how the pecking order is."

"Why don't you give that task to someone else, and we will flip the script."

She nodded to Hilary, who took over purse duty as she led Daniel to the dance floor.

"So, what were you talking about?"

"Well, I've got these friends here, and what we can do is take the focus off of Terry and put it on you."

"Why would you want to do that?"

"Because you deserve it, and Terry always gets all the attention. So, let's ignore her and treat you like a queen."

She had half of a smirk and said, "Why not?"

As the night wore on, he told his friends what was happening, and they followed suit. Each of his friends asked Kristen for a dance, and they all had fun, eventually leaving Terry guarding the purses and fuming. The week went by as a blur, and they went down to the beach and had a grand time. But on the last day of Liberty, Kristen came to his room

with Steve in tow and said, "All right! I've found the one I want, and we can let everything return to normal now."
He looked at Steve, who had this sheepish grin on his face. He nodded in agreement, and they spent the rest of the day by the pool drinking cokes and listening to the portable radio.

Flintknapping

The following day, Daniel awoke early, heard the camp stirring, smelled cooked fish, and felt the warmth of Waisner sleeping next to him. He got up and marched off to water the tree furthest away from the camp and downstream of any flowing water. He scrubbed his hands with sand when his morning ablutions were done and noted their disposition.

Dunes protected The camp on three sides, and some forward-thinking individuals had taken the time to insert sharpened sticks into the top of them in a defensive measure. He walked around the perimeter, noting the features, and saw that the water source was a small stream that ended in a waterfall cascading into a pool one hundred feet away. He heard several voices talking and rounded a grove of trees to come upon fifteen men discussing the finer points of spear-making. "We only have three knives, and we need those to make more weapons." said one tall man with broad shoulders and no neck.

"What weapons have you made?" he asked.

"Spears mostly, sir."

"Any axes or swords?"

"Sir?"

"How about Bows and arrows?"

"We're mostly working with bamboo. Can't do too much with that."

"But there are rocks. Just knap up spear tips, arrowheads, axes, and knives."

"Not following."

"Come with me." He walked them over to the stream and found a rock about the size of a medicine ball. He reached down, pulled it up, and tossed it to the side of a fallen tree. Then he surveyed the area, pointed at three men, and said," Find me some Y branches that would be strong enough to hold a five-pound rock. You two fetch me some vines. We are going to have a class on knapping. Erm..."

"Bowman.", he replied.

"Yes, Bowman. Thanks. I need a rock about the size of a football."

"Coming right up."

A few minutes later, all the materials were laid out before him, and he began by picking up the most vital Y branch and placing it on his knee. Someone passed him a vine, and Bowman gave him the requested rock. "Now we have these two pieces, string them together like so, and wrap the vine back and forth until it's snug. Once complete, we can soak the vines in water, and it will cause them to shrink. So, we take the hammer and use it to swing down onto this rock, and we will see what that gets us. He did so, and the rock split into several pieces. "Now, you can control this as certain rocks have distinct properties and striation patterns that will give you direction on how they should break." There was a piece with a rounded back and a sharp front blade edge. "This will be our ax head." He said as he passed it over to someone who began to fashion it into the tool, much like he had done with the hammer.

"Now, be careful because those ends are wickedly sharp!"

He looked down at the pile of broken rocks and told them, "You have to be able to see what you have, and then you can make what you want. In this case, I have a few pieces that are natural for being arrowheads. Let's put them over here," he said and placed them into a coconut bowl.

"You make that look easy." Said Bowman.

"It's not. I've had lots of practice at it."

"Why?"

"Well, to earn my merit badge and for situations like this. So, we are going to take this piece here," he said, lifting a smooth and rounded chunk on one end about a handspan wide, with a central core that came up and out roughly the length of two fingers. It was shaped like a hammer but with the head flat. "Use it to knap at the pieces we want to shape." He took one of the arrowheads and laid it on the trunk. Then, the knapper was carefully brought down with precise strokes to shape the arrowhead. It left small indentations on the stone, and within a few minutes, the edges were smooth and uniform, and the ends were sharp.

"You don't need to use anything this big; you can get a stone from the creek. You will need one about the size of a robin's egg. Just be careful, as these chips that fly off are sharp."

A hunting party member came running back into the camp breathless and ghost white. Daniel went over to him and handed him a coconut. He was gasping for breath and doubled over with cramps. He drank it and passed it back, nodding thanks. Daniel asked, "What's got you so excited? What did you find?"

"Japs are on patrol. We've killed a boar and brought it back when we noticed them. They were on the other side of the creek from me, and I was told to come back and warn you."

"How many?"

"Half a dozen."

"Waisner."

"On it, skipper! Bowman, bring twenty, all armed, and take them out. But quietly."

"Roger that. He nodded to a group, and they left armed with spears, a few flint knives, and axes."

"Waisner, we're going to need some bows and arrows. Who wants to learn how to make shields?"

An hour later, they had chopped the bamboo down into lengths as long as an arm. He showed them how to align them six by six and weave the vines interlocking. Then, wrap it into two braces, one upper and one lower. He also instructed them to chop the ends into points. Then he demonstrated as he hefted it. Waisner stood opposite, armed with a knife.

"Now we use the shield this way," and pushed forward as Waisner plunged the knife in his direction. The shield caught it, and he twisted it, snapping it out of Waisner's hand.

"Now he's unarmed. I can raise it this way and use the points to slash, stab, and immolate."

The crowd murmured appreciation and went to work in earnest.

An hour later, they had several assembled when the hunting party returned. They trussed the boar on a pole and took it to the fire. They were sporting captured rifles, and Bowman gave Daniel a samurai sword. He asked, "Did they give you any trouble?"

"No, sir. Quick and quiet like you asked."

Looking down at the sword, Daniel said, "Bowman, this is yours; you won it in combat."

"Yes, sir, but that was taken from an officer, so it should be given to one. As you probably know more about its use than I do. I would do more harm than good if I tried to wield it. I'll keep this long knife.", he said, showing the Wakizashi he wore at his hip.

"Good. But we have about two hours before they are noticed as missing. So, we must find their base and see what we're up against. Waisner, you're in charge. Bowman, leave two rifles here, and let's go.

Taking Out the Rising Sun

They left, a ragtag group moving swiftly through the high grass with minimal sound in a fast trot. They came across an animal trail, and he stopped and smeared mud all over his face and exposed areas.

"Sir, what are you doing?" asked Bowman.

"Putting on some camouflage. Plus, it helps to keep the bugs at bay." The weather was broiling, and the temperature was hovering at about 90 degrees. The air smelled of decay as the humidity was so prevalent that one could see it shimmering. Going through the jungle was rough, and they found a small stream after an hour. He told the men not to drink it as it could contain parasites. They used ten minutes to tank up on the coconut water.

The next phase of travel would be through a mangrove swamp. The going was rough as the area was full of black, salty mud that almost pulled you down with every step. They also had to ensure they were not making too much noise and be mindful of poisonous snakes, centipedes, and saltwater crocodiles. After an hour, he could tell that his men were beaten and called a halt for lunch.

"Skipper, there's nothing to eat.", said a sailor.

"There's plenty to eat.", said Bowman.

"Where?" Daniel asked.

"Right here," Bowman said as he approached a piece of fallen wood with tiny holes riddled through it. He picked it up and cracked open the end. The men could see what appeared to be grubs in it.

"What we have here is called a shipworm. But it's just a saltwater clam that likes to bore into wood and eat the fiber.", he said as he reached in and yanked one out. It measured roughly fifteen inches long and was covered in a brownish ooze.

"Looks like a worm," said Daniel as he pulled one out and was prepared to pop it into his mouth, but Bowman stopped him.

"You might want to rinse it off and pinch the shell off the end first."

"Roger that."

One of the men winced as he placed it in his mouth. But he then brightened up. "It tastes like a strong oyster." he declared.

The men began searching earnestly and had eaten their fill in ten minutes. Bowman saw a man plucking a snail off a tree and slapped it out of his hand. Declaring, "NO! Those have to be either roasted or boiled because they contain parasites."

"And what we just ate, didn't?" asked a crewman.

"Nope, because it lives in salt water, and that kills parasites."

"All right people. Good safety tips. Let's press on.", said Daniel. Then, the sky erupted with heavy rain, and Daniel was glad as it would help them get closer to the enemy.

Machine gun fire erupted as they rounded a bend, and two of his men were instantly cut down. The rest dived for cover—half to the left and half to the right of the trail. Daniel could hear screaming, and he saw Bowman dart forward and drag one man off to the side behind some bushes. Then he saw the hidden machine gun nest. It was just a pit with logs thrown over it, with bushes and grass as cover. He and Bowman grabbed the grenades they had gotten from the earlier patrol and tossed them close to the machine gun. Both explosions went off, and they blinded the gunners. His men quickly covered the ground and finished them off.

He bent over to the man who had been hit and saw the wound was pretty bad. "Bowman, see if they have a medical kit."

"Rodger, that Skipper."

He looked down at the fear-stricken face and noticed the man staring at the dead body on the trail. So, he said, "Don't look at him. Look at me. Hey! I said I don't look at him. Look at me!"

The man's attention focused on Daniel.

"I know you're scared, and we are fighting an uphill battle, and you feel like you want to die on this hill. It ain't time for you yet. Don't look at him! LOOK AT ME!!!."

"But sir. It's hopeless. All we got are some rocks and a few rifles."

"This is not going to be the end of you. I know you feel like you've got no strength left. But you need to focus. Listen to me. You are strong. You are capable. You are powerful. The only time you are gonna fail is if you quit. And we don't quit. You're not a quitter. You have made it through 100% of the battles that you have faced thus far. And you are going to make it through this one. Don't look at him. Look at me."

Bowman arrived with the med kit, and someone started working.

"Don't let any doubt infiltrate your mind. Say it: "I am strong. I am capable. I am more than this situation that I am facing."

The acting medic had done all he could.

"Now, pick yourself up. Pick yourself up. You are not finished yet!"

And with that, Daniel walked away. He hears the man groan, and with his help, he gets to his feet.

Bowman said," You are just hurt. Not injured." Then he strode forward to catch up with Daniel.

"How's the inventory?" Daniel asked.

"Pretty good. We got two rifles and a Machine gun. But there's not much ammo left. Also, two bags with rations and some medical supplies."

"Do you think the thunderstorm was enough to cover our ruckus?"

"Gosh, I hope so, Skipper."

Around twenty minutes later, they came to an area devoid of trees with a high fence with concertina wire slung around it. Two guard towers, huts, and small boxes were at the end. A Rising Sun flag was flying high on a pole.

"Bowman, stick to the cover and get me a sitrep."

He nodded, pointed to two others to follow him, and disappeared into the brush. After five minutes, one of the other ranks asked, "What's taking so long?"

Daniel looked at his watch and said," It's only been five minutes."

Half an hour later, Bowman returned with another rifle and a bloodied hand.

"Skipper, they only have about twenty men and are getting nervous."

"Because the patrol didn't return?"

"No, because I cut their radio and about ten feet of wire at different intervals. Should keep them busy for about a day or so.", he said, holding up the strands.

"Let's get back and come up with a plan."

On the return trip, they navigated to the island's north and came across an area devoid of vegetation. Daniel stopped the column by raising his hand and sniffing the air. He smelled death. Bowman came forward. "What's up, skip?"

"This is a graveyard. Fan out and keep your eyes peeled."

They did and quickly found the bodies of prisoners that had been bound so they would strangle themselves if they tried to escape. Then, they had been machine-gunned. After twenty minutes, they counted over ninety bodies.

Daniel's face got so hard and dark that even Bowman was startled. "We are going back to wipe out that camp! NOW!" he barked and took off. They had a hard time keeping up with him. It was dusk when they got back. He sent four groups of five, and they swiftly overpowered those on exterior patrol. He smelled the blood, sweat, and fear, but they pushed on. Next, they entered through the rear gate, and he used the sword to dispatch the guard coming down from the tower on a head run. One stroke, and he was decapitated. A tomahawk was thrown expertly to the skull of the other guard, and he was no more. They carefully and quietly blocked all entrances and exits and rolled a fuel barrel under the main hut. Then, set the place on fire. There was screaming and yelling, and a few even smashed their way out, firing as they came. Two of Daniels's men were killed outright, but the enemy was gunned down.

Daniel found a truck and sent it back to retrieve his wounded. They repaired the radio and reported their position.

The next day, they were situated in the captured camp, but even though they had better facilities and access to medical supplies, three died of their wounds. Waisner told him about it, and he wrote their names down. Remembering that the night before, he had visited them and assured them they would be fine. He started to tear up as he could see Timmy's face as he was relieved about their good fortune. 'I can't wait to be home. This is a million-dollar wound, and I'll be able to marry Shirley.' Now, that would never happen, and he would be buried on some tropical island full of rats and snakes. It wasn't fair. But he couldn't dwell on that right now. He had to get back to the business at hand.

"Okay, so I need to interview everyone to understand better what happened after we got taken out.", Daniel said.

"Well, Skipper, it seems there was a submarine out there that no one was expecting, and that's what got us.

"Is that what also got the Deyrower?"

"No, sir, they had problems with the seam repairs and buckled under the stress of too many hard turns.

"Noted. It's hard to write an after-action report without all the facts."

"Yes, sir, it is."

There was a knocking at the door to the hut. "Come."

The door opened, and a black steward came in with a tray. The aroma made his mouth water. He set the tray down and saw a simple soup with seaweed and a few spoons of rice in a bowl. He noted that the scoop was made of bamboo and was shaped in the traditional oriental style that resembled a longboat. "Sorry to disturb you, sir, but you gotta eat.", he said matter of factly.

Waisner said, "No better place to start your first interview than with Gordon here."

He nodded and motioned for Gordon to sit. He appeared puzzled but complied.

Daniel started the questions around a spoonful of a delectable pork-based broth. "So, tell me, Gordon, how are we on provisions?"

"Not too good, sir. Those Japs were eating worse than we were. That's the last of the white rice. I found a few baskets of rice hulls, some desiccated cabbage, and some grey pudding, but that's all. They seem to have plenty of rice wine and condiments that I can't make heads or tails of.

"I'll stop by the kitchen later and help you with that."

"Okay, sir. But how can you help?

"My wife is Chinese, and I spent some time in the Orient."

"Me too. But I was always below deck. I never really made it to any ports of call. Is that all?"

"For the moment.

He rose and left.

Waisner asked," How long do you think it will take them to send a rescue ship?"

"I don't know. It depends on how badly the battle went, who's in the area, and how far away they are. Why don't you go to the radio shack and see to that?"

"Yes, sir. ", he said as he left.

Daniel returned to his breakfast, or was it lunch?

An hour later, he found Gordon in the kitchen and started to explain what was there. The grey pudding was tofu, a mixture of ground-up beans made into a slurry and steamed. It was very nutritious and used as a meat substitute. There were also some dehydrated mushrooms; they had to pour boiling water over them and wait about twenty minutes. They arranged all remaining ingredients into a large hot pot and made a nice soup to feed all the men, but then they would be totally out of food.

Daniel sent a foraging party out to gather as many snails as possible from the trees. He then sent another group to the beach to collect clams, seaweed, and crabs. That should get them through at least another day.

****

Waisner was in the radio shack when 'Sparky' contacted the coast watchers. There were some tense moments as the codes were verified. This group of individuals had the sole job of keeping watch for Japanese troop movements and relaying information. They used teleradios with a range of 400 miles for voice and 600 miles with Morse code. It would take some time, but they could send word about their situation. They just had to wait for a break in communications to get the word out.

It took two whole days of transmitting and four operators working around the clock to get the list of survivors into the queue. Now, all they had to do was sit and wait.

Pearl Harbor: October 15th, 1943, Memorial Service for the Battle of Bokak Atoll

Kim-Yee was dressed in black along with Hailey, Jack, and Miranda. They sat in the section for the Officer's families, and she noted that there were a lot of widows. She was there as well but didn't feel like one, knowing in her heart that he was missing.

After the service, she sat on the veranda with Hailey while Jack and Miranda napped. "Momma, why do you say daddy's missing, not dead?"

"Because it's the truth."

"But how do you know?"

"I can feel it."

"Why is he missing?"

"Because of the war."

"Why is there war?"

"Because sometimes other people want to control people or covet what they have and then decide to take it. So, people fight back, and then their friends join in, and it goes back and forth."

"When does it stop?"

"When everyone is too tired to care, surrender, or die."

"That's horrible."

"Yes, my darling, it is."

"Is that why Daddy left? To go fight them?"

"Yes."

"But why?"

"Because if he doesn't fight them over there, he might have to fight them here, and none of us wants that. He wants you and your brother to grow up in a free country. To go where you want when you want. To be able to live with who you want and marry them. To vote, learn how to read, write, and do arithmetic. To have the freedom of religion and from religion. To have the right not to be stopped on the streets and searched for no reason."

"But the police came for the Subbayas and took them away. Why? They did nothing; they were a kind elderly couple."

"They were Japanese, and the government feared them."

"So, they took them away and locked them in a camp. How is that freedom?"

"Because they were immigrants and not citizens. They couldn't even own land."

"That's not right, momma."

"And why not, little one?"

"Because if that's the case, why didn't they come for the Germans and Italians? They are at war with us just as much."

"You are learning, child. Probably because they are white and look like them."

"So, if we look different, they fear us?"

"They may."

"It's so wrong."

"Hailey, we are lucky we didn't get swept up in the raids with our neighbors. We are lucky that I was working on the base, and you arrived here before things got ugly. War is ugly. Unfortunately, when people look at you, they will always see a foreigner. It's up to you to convince them they are wrong. You and Jack were both born here, and you have the freedoms and rights granted to you automatically. Your Aunt and I don't."

"Why not?"

"Because we are not citizens yet."

"Why not?"

"It's a process that we must go through called Naturalization, where we must study about America and take a test. Then we can apply for citizenship and, if granted, have to swear ..."

"Swear?"

"Yes, swear, a solemn vow that we have rejected any fealty..."

"Fealty?"

"Yes, loyalty to any other nation. America is now our home; we will protect and defend it with our own lives if necessary."

"But didn't you already do that?"

"Yes, I did during the attack last December. But I was only a nurse, not a member of the military. That came later."

"What came first?"

"Nursing school came first. Where I met a girl named Gwen." Kim-Yee sighed and said, "I had just left Garry, your father."

"Why?" asked Hailey cocking her head slightly to the left as she did automatically when she was thinking.

"Because he beat me," Kim-Yee said, tearing up.

"I didn't know that."

"I know; I didn't tell you."

"Why not?"

"Because I didn't want you to hate him."

"Should I?"

"You must make that decision. I didn't want to poison the well for you with him."

"Why not?"

"Because I wanted you to see him for what he was and for you to decide who he was and how he treated people. I didn't want to rob you of time with your father."

"He's not very nice to people, is he?" she asked crestfallen.

"No. He uses people up. If you have something he wants, he will try to manipulate you to let him have it or give it up. He wants to be able to control people."

"Wow." That was all Hailey could say.

Kim-Yee had a sad smile on her face as she began to tell the tale. Her daughter needed to know that ordinary people can be thrust into extraordinary circumstances. "Now let me tell you about my first day as a Nurse. She had woken to Air Raid Sirens going off. They all stumbled out of their bunks and began to automatically don their uniforms, knowing that some disaster had happened. They spilled out into the quad and heard the drone of aircraft. A bus pulled into the courtyard with an Army Sergeant wearing a sidearm at the wheel. He opened the door and said, "Pearl Harbor is under attack! Get on board if you want to help; we have a mail plane waiting."

The mother Superior nodded and hurried them on board. "Go with God, my children. I will pray for your safety."

He drove like a madman, stopping short of the runway, went to the rear, and grabbed crates, and he and another soldier started loading them. They hurried aboard and found nowhere to sit, heaps and mail sacks. They scrambled over them and dodged the crates being loaded. The hatch shut, and there were two sharp clangs against it, letting the pilot know to take off. He was very young, and his voice trembled as he leaned back and yelled, "Hang on. This is going to be grim!"

Amber, one of the other nurses, could be heard reciting the rosary. They could not see anything outside because this was a cargo plane with no windows. Only the forward windscreen allowed any visual. The pilot gunned the engines and shot forward right to the cliff's edge. Her stomach lurched as the plane dipped and then slowly climbed. They could see massive dots in the sky.

The pilot called out, "Those are not our planes. All the Aircraft Carriers are out to sea. I can hear one of y'all praying back there. You might want to say it louder because if they see us, we're toast!"

Someone started openly weeping, and she called out in a harsh whisper. "Silence! It doesn't help! Keep it together! When we land, it will be in a combat setting; we must move fast to get out of here. He will barely have time to stop."

The next few minutes dragged by, and the silence was excruciating. The pilot started the final approach. "Brace yourselves for an emergency landing! I'll roll to a stop! Y'all jump out and run for the nearest hanger or cover. I'll taxi to safety."

They came in hot and heavy and saw two American Planes on their wings providing cover.

"Angels six and seven, I have 25 guardians on approach. Tell the Hospital they are on their way. The tower is not responding."

"Tower personnel are dead! Stay on the approach five by five. We got you," a male voice said. He was very calm, and then he yelled, "Break right! Do not circle. Land hard. Now!"

The pilot obeyed, making the sign of the cross. They slammed into the tarmac, bouncing and swaying to an abrupt stop. They threw the hatch open and started pouring out. Kim-Yee was counting and came up one short. The pilot was the last out, shoving her forward.

"Where's Gwen?" she yelled.

He yanked her along, screaming, "She's gone! Head for the hanger."

"What?" she yelled in shock, "How?"

"Broken neck!" he slung her to the left as bullets screamed past where they were just a heartbeat ago. They fell into sandbags, and he rolled to the right and headed for a locker. He grabbed a wrench and hammered away until it popped open. He grabbed a BAR-Browning Automatic Rifle and some ammunition, then announced, "Ladies, we made it this far, but those white uniforms are making y'all targets. Change into some coveralls out of the lockers. There are three medical kits in each hanger. One is small and red. That one has morphine. The rest are large and white. I'll find us a ride." He went over to a table with a small radio and turned the dial. He picked up a headset and announced to the fighters that covered their approach, "Angels six and seven, thanks for the assist, 24 guardians safe and sound; one KIA."

"Name of KIA?" Another voice that identified itself as a backup from the tower questioned.

"Gwen," he said and hung up.

He searched the drawer, looking for keys.

One of the Nurses, Le'le, shouted, "Found it." proudly jangling them in her hands.

"Good. Let's load up three or four of y'all on this fire truck. We will go out there and grab as many wounded as possible. Then, bring them back here for triage. I need one of y'all to operate the radio."

Kim-Yee called out, "Becky, radio. Stacey, Alana, and Megan load up. Le'le, you're driving." She felt confident in the choices as Le'le's father ran a trucking company. Becky was a Western Union operator before, and the rest had the highest marks in their classes for trauma.

"Kehlani, you're in charge of triage. The rest of you search for med kits for the hangers and other aircraft." She clapped her hands together and shouted, "Get moving NOW!" She loaded herself into the passenger seat, slapped the door twice, and Le'le put it in gear. They shot off into the fray.

The truck careened onto the tarmac Le'le, dodging left and right to avoid being a target and incoming rounds. They came upon a small group of soldiers and sailors firing at aircraft. All were wounded, but they waved them off. A Gunnery Sergeant yelled, "We're still in the fight! Go help others." He pointed to another sandbag emplacement where they saw a wounded man trying to apply a tourniquet. They drove over, and Alana and Megan jumped off and went into action. She got out, and she and Stacey grabbed a stretcher and loaded him onto it. They got him into the bed between them, and she grabbed the red medkit and ran over to a crashed plane. The tail section was separated, but the gunner banged away at the retreating aircraft. She ran to him and yelled, "Where are you injured?"

He continued firing the double-barreled 50-caliber machine gun and called, "Shoulder!"

She grabbed a styrete of morphine, jabbed him in the leg, and then pinned the tag to the trousers. The gun barrels were bright red, and he ran out of ammo and turned around to let her bandage him up. Once complete, he opened some more cans and started banging away.

She turned and went on to the next wounded. Once full, they roared across the tarmac back to the hanger. They kept the pace up for hours. They didn't have time to think. Just stabilize, get to triage, and load up the ambulances.

When things calmed down, they grabbed a Jeep and went to their crashed plane, where they grabbed the crates of medical supplies. They returned just as a truck arrived, loaded up, and shuttled over to the hospital. The wounded were pouring in from Battleship Row; many were burned badly, and both they and the supplies were dropped off on the lawn. At least they had the foresight to move their Caduceus badges to their collars, so there was no question they were nurses. After several more hours of brutal triage, they were exhausted. A female officer named Gates had approached them as they were scrubbing up. "Girls, thank you very much. I can see that you are all in quite a state. We will go over to the quartermaster and draw fresh uniforms and toiletries. Then to the chow hall, and we should have bunking arrangements made by the time we finish."

They wearily followed her to a waiting truck and went to the chow hall, which served a simple stew over rice. There was bread and jam but no butter. Lemonade, milk, and coffee were available. All ate mechanically, and then they marched over to the quartermaster for a uniform draw; they were issued two stark white uniforms and two powder puff blue with assorted covers, a sweater, underwear, white shoes with rubber heels, and stockings, all of which fit into seabags. Then they loaded onto a truck again and were dropped off at a female barracks. They went in, sorted it out, and showered. Gates showed up as they were about to turn in, "Ladies. We need a list of you and your specialties, and we can develop a roster."

They lined up and stated their names. Gates needed clarification about the spellings, so she handed it back to them to complete. She took the top copy of the roster, left a roll of masking tape and a grease marker, and told them to use it until the name tags were ready.

"You will all have at least eight hours of rest. Keep an eye on the clock. Shifts will be scheduled for 12-hour intervals but could easily drag on to 14-16. The emergency should last no more than three weeks. The uniforms are yours to keep, as we are eternally grateful for your help. Hey, I only have 24 names here. I was told there were 25 of you."

Kim-Yee spoke up, "That would be Gwen. She died during the landing," she said, ending softly.

Gates nodded and asked, "Cause of death?"

"Broken neck." She tried not to cry.

Gates noticed her discomfort and motioned her out into the hall. "Time of death?"

"Around 9?" She said shakily.

Gates tucked her clipboard under her arm, grabbed her by the shoulders, and said, "Honey, you did well. You kept them together, focused, and alive. I've got Nurses, but you are now considered Combat Nurses because you have been through the "Fields of Fire," and no one is a basket case. You are their leader, now officially.

She tucked her head into Gates' arms, who embraced her and said softly, "Let it all out. There, there, you're fine." After several minutes, she held her at arm's length and handed her a kerchief.

"I'm sorry!" she said, almost weeping again.

"No. No. You're crying, not because you are weak. It's because you are human. You've just experienced a great amount of mental and physical trauma. But it would be best if you stayed strong. Don't break down in front of the others."

"How can I do that?" she asked, hiccupping because of the tears.

"I find a supply closet and cry my heart out when necessary. Now, are we good?" Gates said.

"Yes, ma'am," she said. Then she turned around, strode into the barracks, found her bed, and fell asleep instantly. She didn't dream at all. She just slept.

She awoke to the girls chattering away. They looked at the duty roster and a map of the base and saw where they were about the mess hall and the Hospital. Everything was within a few blocks' radii. A Uniform Regulation Training manual was placed at the foot of each bed, where she noticed a locker. A paper clip on the page called "How to wear the uniform smartly."

She read this out loud to them, "Members of the Navy Nurse Corps are required to possess all of the articles of the uniform prescribed except the raincoat as that will be issued on an as-needed basis...Any plain white uniform can be worn if it prescribes the regulation length of skirt and sleeves, white cuff links, the Navy Nurses Corps Cap, plain white stockings, and plain white oxfords with rubber heels. Ward Uniform shall consist of 6 indoor white, three caps, and two pins on markings."

Agnes asked, "Well, they only gave us two of everything, so I guess we are okay, right?"

"Yeah, and if they say anything, ask them to provide what's missing. Now, where was I?" She continued, "Nurses shall always have a watch in good repair on their person. The white uniform shall consist of a skirt attached to the bodice at the waistline and a button-down front with white detachable buttons. The bodice shall be gathered into the waist at the front and back; the skirt shall be gathered into the waist at the back only. A loose belt shall be worn. This uniform shall have a convertible collar three ¼ inches wide at the back and shall be buttoned up to the throat if desired but shall normally be open at the throat. The skirt shall be of a length that conforms to the current length of wearing apparel. (See plate 76)."

Then she went to the billboard and checked the day's Uniform. It said light duty. She consulted the manual and determined it was the blue one. However, some were grey. They all donned their uniforms and checked each other to ensure they presented smartly, and then they all walked to the mess hall and had breakfast. Afterward, they reported to their duty stations. The chaos from the day before had quieted down some, but there was still a sense of urgency. They got instructions from those they were relieving and went to task.

One day, Kim-Yee came around a corner with her hands full and passed by an Admiral. He noticed her, and an aide walked up, asking her for her name and why she didn't salute. She told him, "I have my hands full and am on duty. I have lives to save. Get out of my way," and she went to push past him.

He blocked her and stated sharply, "I need your name, rank, and service number."

She huffed and said, "Chung, Kim-Yee, Nurse, no service number."

"Rank?" he said even more forcefully, "And why are you out of uniform?"

"NURSE!" she replied in kind.

"I can find out your service number," he said smugly.

"No, you can't because I don't have one," she said defiantly.

"Belay that." Admiral Nimitz shot out, "Miss?"

"It's Mrs.," she said, her temper rising.

"Fine, Mrs. Chung. Where are you from?" he asked expectantly.

"Hilo." She said in an exasperated tone.

"Hilo?" he said, thinking quickly," We don't have any bases there."

"No, Admiral, but there is a Nursing School there, and Hilo is not an island. It's a city on the isle of Kona," she said crisply.

"And you are part of the cadets sent over?" he asked carefully.

This sent her over the edge; she placed the items she was carrying on a side table and strode towards him, stating forcefully, "We are not 'Cadets,' we are fully qualified and board-certified Registered Nurses. We flew to your aide during the battle and lost one. We've been working 16-hour days for the better part of a month. The wounded keep pouring in. This hospital was designed for 250 patients; we have over a thousand. We are tired, cranky, and want to go home."

He could see that she was close to tears, making him uncomfortable.

"Then what's stopping you?" he asked, surprised.

"They are!!" she gestured wildly at the rows of injured lining the hallway. "We were told we would only be here for the 'Emergency!' but no relief has come.

"What time do you get off?" he asked.

"EXCUSE ME?" she snarled.

He realized how it came off and was stammering an apology, "No! Not like that. What time can you drop by my office so we can get to the bottom of this?"

"Oh...no, you don't!" she said, setting her face for battle. "We've been promised left and right that someone would take care of this. I'm not letting you out of my sight until then!" She hooked her arm in his and stated fiercely, "Wherever you go. I go until this is resolved!"

He called after the aide, "Have Mrs. Chung excused from her duties on my authorization." He turned and escorted her to the waiting car. "My office," he barked to the driver.

They went inside, and he asked her to sit down. Then he got on the phone and had several more brought in. Coffee was served, and he requested tea for her. She was so tired she passed out. When she awoke, he sat on the edge of a desk with a large legal pad and a different aide handing him documents.

Hailey interrupted, "Wow! Mom! You stood up to Admiral Nimitz?"

"Yes, dear. I had to. It was the only way to get things done; I was only a civilian volunteer who had been pressed into service. What was the worst that they could do to me? Ask me to leave?"

"So, then what happened?"

"Then the Admiral and I figured out what had been going on. He woke people up and got records and duty rosters pulled. I had fallen asleep, and when I awoke, he had a vague picture of what had transpired. "Okay, here's what I've gathered so far. When you landed, you were called Mercy Flight 7 with 25 guardians on board. You list one dead, and it was recorded. You all did emergency medicine triage on the runway at Hickam and were sent to the main Hospital. Afterward, you were put under the command of Captain Gates. She got you all fed, clothed, and billeted. Then, she established a duty roster and was given orders to report to the Hospital ship Potemkin for duties in and around the Coral Sea. You then fell under the command of Colonel Means, who was also shipped out on the same hospital ship. We lost several nurses in the attack, and you just happened to fill in the gaps because you all kept to the duty roster without fail. No one knew you were civilians, and because of the crush of patients, military uniform standards went out the wayside. Hence where we are today."

"Then to whom do we report?" She asked.

"Well, to no one, but ultimately to me," he said.

"What are you going to do about it?" She wiped her eyes, poured herself some more tea, and rose to fill his.

"Well, first things first. You all need to be paid, and we've been overworking you all, so I've authorized the paymaster to give you double the standard rate of military nurses. This is a one-time deal. Half can be returned to your families immediately; you may draw the other half in person. I also learned about a Cadet Nursing Program; my staff thought you were part of it. Yet another reason you all slipped through the cracks. But that's for untrained personnel. I want to hire all of you and put you into service as a Home Guard and Ready Reserve Nurses Corp. You will not leave the Hawaiian Islands. What do you think about that?" he asked.

"I think I'm the wrong person to be talking to about that," she said frankly.

"Well then, let's talk to your fellow Nurses about it," he said excitedly.

"No. We need to fly to Hilo and talk to Mother Superior about it," she said.

"Why?"

"Because they paid for our education, and we have responsibilities to the communities we trained for."

He felt sucker-punched, and he should have thought of it. "Okay, just let me get a couple of things straightened out, and then we will go." He lifted the phone, said, "Get me a flight to Hilo and amend that letter of intent with the following information..." and rattled it off. She gathered herself, and they walked out of the office, down the hallway, out the door, and down the steps to the waiting car. "Airfield.," he said.

They boarded the plane several minutes later, and she was seated across from him. The leather seat was luxurious, and the appointments were lavish. Coffee was served, and he pulled out a flask and poured some in. He offered her the flask, and she took it and gave it a healthy pull, then handed it back. He was impressed with this 5'1" ball of fury. The flight was uneventful, with zero turbulence, and it was over before she could get used to it. They landed and disembarked. No car was waiting. Not even a Jeep. A soldier called out from a guard hut. "Come in here to warm up, sir." It was windy and cold. But the shack was warm. It had a hot plate with a boiler of coffee on it. There was a tin for bread and a toaster.

"I'm afraid all I can offer you is some coffee and toast. They just woke up and are fueling a car for you. But the crisp air causes moisture, so they need to decant it properly. Otherwise, it could gum up."

"Coffee and toast sound great!" he said as he grabbed a cup and poured himself one. He offered her some, but she refused. The guard charged the toaster, and when it popped up into the air, he caught it expertly with the plate. He handed it to her with a smile, and she passed it to Nimitz. He noticed she was shivering, so he gave her a watch cloak. She took it gratefully and nodded thanks.

They heard a horn honking later and climbed into a three-seater Bantam Jeep. It had no cover. Nimitz moved the passenger seat, and Kim-Yee climbed into the back.

"What's the name of the place where we are going?"

"Sacred Heart Nursing School," she said.

The driver shrugged.

It's off the Queen Lille o Kalani Highway, the large white building that looks like a hospital?" she spoke.

"Oh, that one. Got it," and the driver peeled out.

They drove through the darkness and saw the early morning dawn, and as they pulled in and went into the courtyard, they noticed all the buildings were dark.

"Are they awake?" Nimitz asked.

"Yes. They have just finished prayers and should be coming out about now," she said as heavy wooden doors opened and lamplight spilled out, carving its amber glow through the darkness.

She jumped out and ran towards an older woman in a nun's habit.

"Mother Superior," she said excitedly as she embraced her.

"Are you back, child? Where are the others?" she asked, surveying the empty courtyard.

"Not quite," she said as she turned and motioned for Nimitz to join them.

"This is Admiral Nimitz," she said, introducing him.

"What happened to the other one?"

"I replaced him," he said.

"Come. We are just going to break bread. Get out of the cold. Join us." She turned towards the kitchen hearth.

He followed them and sat at the long wooden table. Finger bowls were set, and all stood. Heads were bowed, and the prayer of thanks was given. He saw fresh pineapple, a large chunk of bread with butter and honey, a boiled egg, and a Stein of beer. Good.

They ate, and he let them get caught up. He enjoyed the meal and the silence. They talked among themselves but in hushed, reverent tones. All the sisters had a sense of grace and calm reverence about them. He could tell that they were patient but also stern. He waited for recognition, kept quiet, and enjoyed the meal.

"I'm sorry, Admiral. We were just getting caught up. Tell me, have you found Gwen's body?"

"Gwen?" he asked.

"Yes, the nurse who died upon the crash landing. That one," she said flatly.

He pulled out a small notebook and jotted it down, stating, "I'll have to get back to you on that."

"When will I get my Nurses back?" she asked.

"That's a little more problematic..." he started.

"Really? Why?" She asked, raising one eyebrow.

"Because we still have over 4,000 wounded and are running out of places to put them," he said.

"Then send the convalescence cases to us. That should alleviate some of the pressure. There are several nursing homes around the islands as well. Some abandoned estates could be shifted to this measure, providing you send resources to help. We have Nursing Assistants and Nursing Students that could use the practice."

"That all sounds fine and good," he said, writing it down. "But I need to keep your nurses for the time being."

"I'm afraid that is just not possible. They have duties and obligations that have been unfulfilled for a month," she said, her tone getting slightly sharp.

"Mother Superior, I have a letter from the President of the United States of America that authorizes me to acquire all resources necessary for the war effort. This includes trained personnel. I would rather not use it. Instead, I offer a partnership. Now, normally, how many Registered Nurses can you crank out annually? 25?"

"That's correct."

"How about if we provide you with the resources to turn out over 150?" he asked excitedly.

"That's preposterous. We don't have the means," she began.

"We could provide it," he said as she rose and walked down the hall. She was swift, and he raced to catch up to her.

"I'm all ears," she said as they came to her office and sat down.

He was not used to being on this side of a desk, which would be a hard sell. "A Registered Nurse takes 36 months to train, right? We have developed a curriculum that brings it down to 30 months. There is also an LPN course that takes half the time. We might even be able to get it down to one year. And a Nursing Assistant cohort that takes six months; therefore, if we follow your logic and purchase or rent these abandoned estates and upfit them, then run separate revolving cohorts running day and night, we should be able to have candidates regularly."

"That won't work—the two shifts. Everything else sounds reasonable, and if we run on Saturdays and year-round, we might be able to accommodate. Plus, we have several cohorts running already. I would need to see the accelerated curriculum to plan to crash the current cohorts into compliance. However, that still doesn't explain how we house all these additional students. Then we would need more labs, classrooms, library space, and instructors."

"All could be constructed, rented, or up-fitted," he said.

"How about my nurses; what are your plans?" she asked.

"I want to hire them. But it's entirely voluntary. We would also pay you twice their training costs. I have a check for you to fill out regarding that," he said.

"And if they don't want to work for you?"

"Then their obligations stand, and I will send them back," he said.

"So, how will we solve the problem of the communities they were supposed to serve?"

"We will establish clinics in those communities and make it part of the training."

"Why would you want LPNs over RNs?" She asked.

His mind was racing to keep up when Kim-Yee, sensing he was out of his depth, cut in, "It takes half of the time, and the jobs are quite different. If you let the RNs manage the LPNs, you have a more elegant and effective care cycle. The LPNs can care for routine needs, and the RNs can run IVs and administer medication."

"And the Nursing Assistants, why are they necessary at all?" Mother Superior asked.

Kim-Yee answered, "Because they can take care of order filling of supplies, observation, meal service, general wound, and dressing care. Filling each category allows for the greater care of more patients. Thus alleviating the pressure and allowing the higher trained personnel more time for critical care needs."

He just smiled and nodded.

"Once trained, I don't want them to disappear into the military machine; what kind of safeguards are you offering?" Mother Superior asked.

"They will be sworn in as a Home Guard/Reserve Nursing Corps for the Territory. They will not leave the Hawaiian Islands. I have it in writing." he said.

"I wish to see both letters," she asked.

"Here you are," he said as he passed them over.

She took the first one, then turned around and placed it into the potbelly stove.

"I like this one better," she said as she rose. "Well then, let's be on our way."

"To where?" he asked.

"Why to Pearl." she said, "I need to see my girls." They went to the courtyard. She walked towards the Jeep and grabbed an apple crate, which she used to climb aboard, then reached down and retrieved it and set it down. He was impressed. Now he saw where Kim-Yee got her character from. They went back to the airfield and climbed aboard, then took off.

Once they landed, they were whisked away in the car to the Nurse's barracks. She met with them and came out with three Nurses with packed musette bags after about an hour. "These three don't wish to remain. They are married and want to stay with their communities in Hilo. I will draft you a check for the difference."

"Not necessary. Use the funds to hire an architect and at least three handymen. Their first project should be to build their housing. Then, acquire the buildings you need and enough supplies to get you started. Send your requirements to my office, and we will get work crews and supplies to you. You may take my car," he said as the driver came out to help load the bags.

"Now what?" Kim-Yee asked.

"Now we will get you all sworn in and into an officers training cadre," he said. "It shouldn't take more than 30 days."

She thanked him, saluted, and went to her barracks.

"So, what happened to your friend Gwen?"

"They found her in a morgue a few weeks later, and Admiral Nimitz promised he would give her a memorial service. I will follow up with him because she must be remembered."

Gwen

"I have told you of my first day as a nurse. Now, let me tell you about my first day as a nursing student. Your auntie and I had been living together for some time, with me working as a waitress, and we were crammed into a small bungalow, but we didn't care. She could do her accounting business anywhere. I had applied to several schools and was nervously awaiting a response from any of them. The application fees were not much, but even $5 can be the difference between having a good month and a bad one. Hilo's practical nursing program was my best chance to change our circumstances. I received that letter, and they even sent a ferry ticket. They offered me a scholarship if I agreed to work it off over three years. I jumped at the chance and packed a bag. You all went with me to the ferry terminal, and as I boarded, I noticed a young redhead who looked as lost as I was. She juggled too many items, and her purse fell to the deck. An orange rolled out, and I picked it up and handed it to her. She was wearing glasses and dressed so stylishly in a pretty polka-dotted dress.

"Thanks.", she said, smiling, her face turning slightly pink in embarrassment. "You keep it. I have more, and this ride will take a while. I'm Gwen."

"Kim-Yee. I noticed you have the catalog for Sacred Heart Nursing School courses." I'm going there too."

"I just got accepted as well. The mail is running slow."

"Me too. Barely made it in time for the ferry."

She was a lovely girl from a good family and always had her head in a book. She didn't chase any boys and seemed to fly under their radar even though she had a good figure and was likable. "So, where was I?"

"The ferry," said Hailey with a slightly sad smile as she saw her mother work through the pain of a friendship cut short on that horrible day not so long ago.

"Yes. The ferry. We safely made it to the dock, where a bus awaited us. We loaded up and went to the school. When we arrived, they set up tables in the courtyard and had a nice lunch for us. We were to mingle and get to know each other for over two hours. Then, we were to declare if we had any choices for roommates. Of course, we chose each other and thus began a lifelong friendship. Unfortunately, her life was cut short. We were inseparable. We spent hours on coursework and studying in the library. If something didn't make sense, she would say, "Put it away, and let's go outside, enjoy the sunshine, and go for a walk. It will still be there when we get back."

"She had such optimism and then died on final approach during an attack. It's just not right!" she said, her voice turning hard. She stood up and went to the telephone. "Operator, get me Admiral Nimitz's office. It's Kim-Yee."

"He's swamped."

Her voice got hard and cold. "Listen to me very carefully. I need to speak with him Now!"

"Yes. Yes, M'am!"

A very tired-sounding voice came on about a minute later," Kim-Yee. I don't have any news..."

"That's not what I'm calling about. Remember your promise to find out what happened to Gwen?"

"Of course."

"Well?"

"We found her and have put together a memorial service but were waiting on Congressional Approval."

"For what? She was a civilian."

"Yes, she was. Now listen to me closely. You can't divulge this to anyone else." She smiled conspiratorially and motioned for Hailey to come listen to the phone. "Go on. I promise." she almost squealed in laughter.

"We put you all in for the Congressional Gold Medal. That is the highest honor that can be awarded to a civilian. The approval just came through. It will be at the quad on Sunday at noon. We couldn't get a hold of her family."

"I'll stand in for her, Admiral.", said Hailey.

"Well, I'll be. Taking after your mother, I see. Okay, sport. It's a date. Sunday at Noon."

"Mother, I thought you said Gwen came from a good family," Hailey asked.

"Yes. She did. Why?"

"Had you ever met them?"

"Why do you ask?"

"Because it seems weird that the military couldn't locate her family. Seeing as how they are very meticulous when it comes to records."

"I see your point. What do you want to do about it?"

"I want to try and find out all I can about Gwen."

So, Kim-Yee called the courthouse and asked about the birth and death records. Then they both went down there and looked up at Gwen. She was born in the Hawaiian Islands of Niihau, known as the "Forbidden Island." The clerk gave Hailey a pamphlet that explained the small island. 'Less than 200 people live in a small village called Pu'wai. It is eighteen miles southwest of the Island of Kauai, known as Garden Island. A small naval facility is on the island, and ferries run to and from Kaua'i. The natives live off the land and hunt and fish for sustenance.'

"Wow, Mom, that sounds like a neat place to live."

"Yes, my dear, it does. Let's get some tickets and take a ride over."

"Okay."

So, they walked down to the Pier, and Kim-Yee bought Hailey a snow cone and herself a lemonade while they waited. The ferry ran a circuit; the last one off the island would be at dusk. They enjoyed the swiftness of the ferry and the cool breezes that came with the ride.

They disembarked and walked to the village. They asked around the general store about Gwen, and nobody seemed to know who they were talking about. Finally, Kim-Yee got mad and roared in the market square. "Does anyone not know a curvy redhead that was born and raised here?"

One of the elders working on making a lei out of seashells stopped what he was doing and rose, motioning them over.

"I knew that young girl. Always curious and getting into mischief. She was not bad-natured; she was just overly curious and would end up in trouble because she was a bit clumsy. What is your purpose for being here?"

"I'm Kim-Yee, and this is my daughter Hailey. Gwen was my best friend in Nursing School, and she died in the attack on Pearl Harbor. The government would give her a Medal Posthumously, but they could not locate her parents. So, we came here hoping someone could point us in the right direction."

He pointed to a small cemetery. "That is the right direction." He stood and slowly walked them over to two headstones leaning against each other. "These two were her parents. Inseparable. So much so that they both died within a few days of each other. She is from Eclampsia, and he is from Scarlet Fever. We had to burn their house down for the safety of the village. So, we placed their ashes in tins and made small headstones for them. But as you can see, they are inseparable.

"Gwen was an orphan?"

"Not quite. She had an uncle who treated her decent, but we had to intervene when she was about 11 or 12 and started to show her womanly figure. We passed her from family to family for as long as we could, but then the Government got wind and came and took her away to a convent school."

Hailey knew that the elder was talking about things and made a mental note to ask her mother about the importance of what was not being said.

They thanked him for his time, and he leaned over and presented the lei to Hailey. She bowed in acceptance and was delighted as the shells were lovely. Kim-Yee tried to pay the man, but he would have none of it. "You were her Ohana, as were we. It is only fitting that you take this lei to her funeral."

As they returned to the pier, Hailey asked her mother what was on her mind. "Mom, why was he talking in circles?" she asked.

"Because you were present, and he wasn't sure if what he thought was true. As it was just a suspicion."

"What was suspected?"

"That her uncle was not very nice to her and might have abused her."

"Like beat her?"

"Yes, and maybe more."

"Like what?"

"Like he might have been touching her."

"Why would an uncle do that?"

"Not everyone is raised the same way, and some men treat all women as objects to be conquered. I wouldn't say I like this subject, but as a young woman now, you also need to be very cautious around men. Not all are bad; some will try to exploit you."

"Like what?"

"Like maybe brushing up against you, cupping your breast, or touching your rear end."

"Wouldn't that be creepy?"

"Yes. And it will make you uncomfortable. Generally, you can see it in their eyes as they leer.."

"Leer?"

"Yes, they might give you a look like this." as she did her best impression of a man leering."

Hailey giggled, "Mom. Stop being silly."

"I'm not a young lady. This is serious. Trust me, when a man gives you that look, you can almost feel it. It's almost like someone saying in a rough voice, 'FRESH MEAT!'"

"Okay, now that is creepy."

"Yes, it is. But it can almost start innocently. Like boys giving you a wolf whistle."

"What's that?"

"It's like this," as she pursed her lips and made the 'wheet whew' sound.

"OH! So that's what that means."

"So, you've heard it?"

"Yes. At school. Some of the boys were whistling, and one of the girls shot them a look, and they stopped. I didn't think anything of it at the time."

"Then, as they get closer to you, they might want to maybe brush a lock of hair out of your face, and they might lean in and close their eyes as they cup your cheek and try to kiss you."

"Eeew, gross."

"Good answer. Don't ever let anyone do anything to you. Your body is your own, and if a boy respects you, he will ask to hold your hand."

"Sounds like dangerous times."

"It can be, but you are lucky as we live on the base, and most of the young men there are from good families and raised with manners. But if a boy gets fresh with you, I want you to slap him in the face as hard as you can. Make a scene. Sat very loudly, 'Don't you get fresh with me!' If he continues, I want you to punch or kick him in the groin."

"Ouch!"

"Yes, but very necessary. If he persists, the scream for help, yelling 'RAPE!', generally works. Other men should come to your aid. If that doesn't work, run into the middle of the street and stop a car. Throw a rock at the windshield if you need to. I know this sounds extreme, but it puts your life at risk. If none works, prepare to defend yourself: scratch, claw, and bite. Please take off your shoes and use the heels to beat at them. Go for the eyes and the head. Slap them so hard in the ears that it messes with their equilibrium. Make it too expensive so they don't want to mess with you. Remember that males are larger and stronger than you. Always be aware of your surroundings. If you think that you are being followed, go into a store. If the person following you is hanging around and waiting for you, have the store call the police."

"Here's the ferry.", Hailey said as they saw it pull in and snug up to the docks. The ramp was lowered, and they went aboard. They had their tickets in hand but were not asked to show them since the same crew had dropped them off. The team started working on the cargo that they had brought. The goods were transferred, and within thirty minutes, a pile of crates with Navy markings was on them. They saw a truck pull up, and sailors in blue chambray work uniforms wearing white covers disembarked. They strode purposefully towards the stack, all having their shirt sleeves rolled up. All were sporting tans, and a few had exposed tattoos. One of them was wearing chevrons, and he was obviously in charge. Within fifteen minutes, all the crates were transferred to the waiting truck, and the men climbed aboard a second one and drove away back to their small base. Some of the men smiled up at Kim-Yee and Hailey, and they waved good-naturedly at them. Then the ship's horn was sounded, and the diesel engines chugged as the ferry was put into full reverse. At about three lengths of the vessel, they started to turn away from the shore and back home. They both enjoyed the sunshine and got lost in their thoughts. She asked how to be more aware of the tricks men or boys might pull. Her mother is over the sadness of her friend's life.

****

The next day, Hailey was up at the crack of dawn and wanted to go to the orphanage to see if they could find more information about Gwen. "Aren't we done with that?" her Mother asked.

"No. If I speak on her behalf, I need to know her."

"Okay. Let's get some breakfast first."

They went to the kitchen and started to prepare bacon and eggs with grits, toast, jam, and coffee. Kim-Yee fixed Hailey a cup of mostly milk with a lot of sugar. "Here, try this. It's called French style."

Hailey lifted it to her lips and blew on it to cool it down. Then she took a tentative sip and grinned."

"Do you like it?"

"Yes, Mom. Thanks."

"Why aren't you having any?"

"I don't like it. Too bitter. I'll stick to tea."

Later on, they washed up and got dressed.

"Today, we will take the bus as Miranda needs the car for shopping."

They walked to the bus stop and got tickets to the middle of town, where the main terminal was.

After two more stops and transfers, they were at the school. It was a nondescript white stucco building with a dormitory, a library, a gymnasium, a church, gardens, and outbuildings.

Hailey hesitated as she got off the bus.

"Lead on. This is your adventure."

She did and marched up to the door and met with the secretary. Telling her the mission and what she hoped to get out of it. The nun was very kind and told her, "Just wait at that table over there, and I will be right with you."

Sister Cynthia walked off, went to a few shelves, and pulled down a few small books and a few larger ones. Then came over and sat down. She opened the larger text, and Hailey saw it was a yearbook. "Gwen was one of our brightest. She had a very sharp and curious mind. So much so that she got into trouble quite often."

"What kind of trouble?"

"Just the kind when you speak out of turn or challenge authority. Those two were her specialties. There was no malice in it. Just that sometimes her mouth got ahead of her brain.", she said wistfully.

"What else can you tell me about her?"

"She had a rather large appetite and loved meat and potatoes. She was also quite fond of fruit and loved to read books about adventure."

"What kind of books?"

"Oh, the usual. Treasure Island. Moby Dick. Little Women was one of her favorites."

"I see. How long was she here for?"

"Several years."

"Did she ever get adopted?"

"Yes, twice, but it didn't work out."

"Why not?"

"The first adoption was by a nice older couple, but we could tell that the adoption was the wife's project. She left around thirteen and returned at fifteen when the missus died. The husband was apologetic about it, saying she was a good girl and caused no trouble, but he had come down with cancer and would be dead in a few months and felt that it would be best to bring her back. She hugged him and returned to us, very sad."

"The next adoption was okay, but the couple was fighting all the time and soon got divorced, so she came back again and stayed. She aged out of the system and was hired by the school to help teach some younger ones."

"How could she do that?"

"Well, let's see.", Sister Cynthia said as she pulled out a certificate. "This here is a correspondence course."

"What does that mean?"

"It means that she was mailed a course of study, and she had to purchase the book that went with it and accomplish the tasks, then mail them in upon completion. If any tests are to be taken, they must be under controlled conditions, signed by a school administrator, and witnessed."

"Ah,"

"As you can see, she got high marks and finished quite quickly."

"Why wouldn't she just go to college?"

"Hailey, some schools are not for everyone, and some circumstances don't lend well to the normal course of study."

"I see. So, this type of learning worked best for her?"

"Yes. It did. So much so that she could apply to nursing school; that was the last we saw of her."

" I wish that I had something of hers to read at the memorial service.", Hailey said dejectedly.

Sister Cynthia pulled out a keepsake book and gave it to Hailey. "This might help you in your journey to understand Gwen."

They thanked her for her time and left. Sister Cynthia gave them both hugs and dried her tears with a handkerchief. They gathered up their things and departed.

****

Time passed quickly, and on Sunday, they were at yet another memorial service, but this was more uplifting as they celebrated life and the camaraderie of twenty-five young nurses who put their lives on the line to help others.

There was a large picture of Gwen in her nurse's uniform. It was a graduation shot, and Kim-Yee smiled and noted that she would be forever young in their eyes. The ladies were all called one by one to receive their medals. Then Gwen's name was called, and Hailey received it in her place. Her mother had found an old journal entry that Gwen had made and dutifully copied it for her to read. "My name is Hailey, and I am here instead of Gwen, who earned this medal; she was my mother's best friend. I have something here that Gwen wrote in a journal.

'Time waits for no man.

No woman, either.

It chews up mountains and wears down rivers.

But it flows on and on, and in a lifetime, if we can be remembered, that is good enough. We are truly alive if that memory is passed down through the ages. We flow on into the either.

Ashes to ashes and dust to dust.

She went and sat back down. There was not a dry eye among them. Nimitz took the podium and made a motion, and an honor guard came in bearing a coffin draped with an American flag. "It's with a heavy heart that I stand before you. Gwen will receive full military honors as she came to our aid in our time of need. The honor guard carefully and respectfully folded the flag and handed it to Nimitz, who solemnly passed it to Hailey as the 21-gun salute went off in the background. She flinched once because she was not expecting it. She steeled herself for the subsequent two volleys. Nimitz sat down next to her, totally exhausted emotionally. Hailey leaned against him, guessing correctly that even men need comfort.

Later, they were at the reception at the O-Club, and she asked Nimitz about her dad. He told her that they had received reports of fifty survivors from the battle; while he didn't have a list of names yet, he went to the office and "Kick some tail until he did." He made his apologies and left.

Kim-Yee walked up and asked. "What were you and the Admiral talking about?"

"Oh, that? Just about, Dad."

"What did he say," she asked, genuinely puzzled.

"Just that he was returning to the office to Kick some tail! Until he found out.

The Rescue

The topography of Bokak Atoll was much the same as the rest of the island chain. It was composed of a buildup of a coral reef atop a long-dormant volcano. The shape of these is either triangular or horseshoe. Bokak was the latter. Their body helps to make a lagoon that is naturally protected from the elements and only has a few approaches through narrow channels, which makes them excellent natural fortifications.

The value of this real estate to the Navy is priceless as its shape lends itself to easy conversion to airstrips, and the coral provides most of the resources necessary to create runways. The deep water of the lagoon makes it an excellent place for anchorage.

The Japanese troops reinforced the natural defenses by building a coconut log sea wall with machine gun nests and firing steps aimed at the lagoon.

From his vantage point up in a guard tower, Daniel could see all of this, and he had lookouts stationed to keep any enemy from sneaking up on them. They noted the location of several bunkers and possible fuel dumps and called them into the spotters. They also stated that in the lagoon, several sets of defenses were arranged with concrete pyramids to keep tanks from easily landing and barbed wire set into the coral reef that caused any approaching troops to be funneled into the waiting machine guns. He climbed down and was relieved by a watchstander. "Keep a sharp eye out and let me know if anything changes."

"Roger that, sir."

He went on daily rounds to check the camp's status and the men. Sparky told Wiesner that he heard a lot of chatter in Japanese and thought they might expect an attack. He started sending out an S.O.S. immediately, and it was relayed.

"They are about three hours out.", he said.

"Who? The Japs or our rescue?"

"Both"

"Roger that." He turned and sprinted to the commandant's office, yelling, "Skipper!"

Daniel looked up from his interview with the Doctor and said, "What's going on?"

"Two problems. The Japs are on the way, and so is the rescue party."

"And?"

"They will probably arrive at the same time. They know the lay of the land, and our boys don't. What do we do?"

"Oh, that's duck soup, Wiesner. Just load up the truck with fuel, and then we will prep the most logical avenues of attack and light them if they get too close."

"I'll make it happen." he left the hut and yelled, "Bowman. I need five strong men, all armed with rifles and hand grenades. We've got a mission."

About two hours later, twenty aboriginal tribesmen arrived to reinforce them. They were friends of the Coast Watchers Brigade.

They set the trap and waited. They could hear and feel the barrage of navy guns as their comrades fought their way ashore. Daniel was up in the tower again and saw quite the task force of several destroyers, two light cruisers, a small flattop carrier, multiple support craft, and a hospital ship. The planes from the airline roared overhead, and the men cheered. Daniel could see the landing craft launching fast approaching the beaches. Waisner was antsy, and he said, "Spit it out!"

"Well, sir, maybe we should find a way to help them out there."

"No way. We've done our part. We've got the information and relayed it. All we can do is sit tight, as we are essentially combat ineffective. We've got too many wounded, and even if we tried, those left behind would be completely defenseless."

Waisner looked down sheepishly, "I know, sir, but it still feels like we're doing nothing."

"Well, there's laying low and being smart about it. That's what we are doing."

Then, they heard rumbling and the sound of tracked vehicles. The tribesmen were armed with shields and spears hidden in the tall grass. The enemy had no idea of what was in store for them. They unthinkingly moved parallel to a truck, followed by a tiny tank. Suddenly, the Aboriginals melted out of the grass, and each took a man down. One swift strike, a crunch, thud, or squelch, and it was done. Because of the noise of the tank, no one noticed, and they blended back into the tall reeds.

Then a shot rang out. It was on! His men had stripped the dead of their weapons and began to fight back. The truck stopped, troops began pouring out, setting up a firing line, and then the fuel was lit. They were in the perfect spot and were standing right in the puddle. There was screaming and a loud boom. The tank rolled up, and it was ablaze. A foot kicked out a plate, a man came out on fire, and he was shot dead. Then, the steady drum of a multi-barreled 50 caliber started tearing into the remaining attack force, and they heard the LVT (Landing Vehicle, Tracked) come into view through the underbrush. It was an Amphibian Tractor known as an 'amtrac,' but the troops generally called it an alligator. This was a lightly armored personnel carrier that could hold about twenty men. Its top speed was about four knots in the water, and it could roll right over most obstacles up to chest height. They were great in this theater of war as the coral reefs provided no challenge. On land, they had a top speed of twenty miles per hour. It laid down a lethal barrage of lead, and the surviving attackers ran for it and right into the Ready Reaction Force of Marines and were cut down to a man. Then, the Marines methodically went through each body and riddled it with more bullets. Daniel saw this from the compound gate where they had thrown together a rudimentary barricade of empty barrels, some felled trees, a cart, and multiple sandbags. As he thought the battle was over, there was a barrage of weapons fire from the underbrush. Four men went down instantly, and he felt something slam into his skull. His body went slack as he fell backward over a sandbag. He was extremely relieved; surprisingly, there was no pain. The LVT drove up to the gate, and they were opened. Troops and medical personnel were disgorged, and the Exodus began. Everything then went black.

Then, they were all evacuated to the hospital ship, where delousing and medical evaluations were performed. He awoke an untold number of hours later on an operating table. He felt a slight tug and jumped up, swinging his arms. Bodies were thrown across his, and he smelled the sweet smell of ether as he passed out again.

He awoke in a wheelchair outside of the Captain's quarters. His body felt numb, and he could only see from one eye. His name was called, and he met with the Captain and Head Surgeon, where he turned in his After-Action Report and debriefed. He informed them of the tactic that he had used to take the camp, and they noted it, but that was all. He expected some fallout or disgust at the warning, but there was no reaction. He inquired about it, and they asked him if he observed the Marines making sure every enemy on the battlefield was dead several times over. He answered in affirmative, and the Captain said, "We are not taking any prisoners. They are untrustworthy in their acts of surrender as they believe they must kill as many of us as possible. Therefore, we use flame throwers as often as possible to mitigate their effective neutralization. It seems you found another way to achieve these same goals. You are to be commended on your actions, which will be reflected on your record. Thank you for your service. You stand relieved. Rest up. It will be a few weeks until we get back to Pearl. You may use my day cabin and have priority access to the radio shack.

The Head Surgeon remarked. "You are one tough cookie. That machine gun round clipped you good. A millimeter one way or the other, and you would have died. But it just glanced off that hard head of yours."

Daniel was wheeled back to the assigned quarters, and a corpsman helped him into the bunk. He was asleep before his head hit the pillow, dead tired. He was drained both physically and emotionally. When he awoke, he had no idea how much time had passed, but he saw that a tray of coffee, milk, juice, and toast had been set. So, he swung out of bed and had breakfast. He knew he had to eat slowly and carefully to not shock his body. The coffee was still warm, and it soothed his parched throat. The milk was still cold as a few ice cubes had been placed in the glass, and he enjoyed the crispness. Then he fell upon the toast and relished the real butter. Next, he finished off the orange juice and wiped his mouth with the linen napkin provided.

He saw that a fresh uniform had been laid across the opposing chair and donned it. I noted that he had lost a few pounds, which didn't quite fit. So, he went out to find the tailor shop.

Next, he worked his way over to sick call and waited his turn on the red bench. One sailor came out rubbing his groin with a look of sheer anguish. The doctor on call had his back to him and was filling out a sick card for the previous patient. He swung pleasantly and said, "So what seems to be the ..." Gulp, "Problem?"

"Is it that bad, doc?" asked Daniel.

"Let me see," he said as he reached over to remove the eye patch. He did so and was rewarded with seeing Daniels's left eye fully swollen shut.

Daniel could also see it from the mirror that he was facing. He noticed that half of his head had been shaved, and he had what appeared to be over fifty stitches from the top of his left eye to the rear of his ear.

"Oy, I can see how that looks. Pretty Grim.", said Daniel.

The doctor reached for a long syringe and filled it with a clear flask. As he leaned forward, Daniel leaned back.

"Hold on there. It's just saline. I need to wash the wound and rinse the crusty bits."

Daniel snickered," Is that a medical term there, doc? Crusty bits?"

"Well, it gets the point across. Plus, I need to check and ensure the Iris and Cornea are intact. I don't want you to get a secondary infection and lose it."

"Ok. I give. Go ahead"

After the eye was rinsed and the crusty bits removed with a cotton swab on a long wooden stick. He looked down and saw what the doctor had feared—a green, sickly-looking bit of puss. Doc noted Daniels's face was going white.

"Don't worry." I'll give you some anti-septic. But first, I need to numb it locally. I need to get some help. Corpsman?" he yelled down the hall. Daniel heard feet running, and a Corpsman dressed in all white arrived breathless a few seconds later. "Yes, sir?"

"Get me the head immobilizer, paracetamol, anti-septic wash, and a spare body."

"Aye, sir."

Five minutes later, he arrived with the requested items and a large Marine.

"Okay, Skipper, here's what we are going to do. We need to immobilize your head and freeze your eyeball. Then we need to numb it, and I'll work on removing that stray piece of copper jacketing they missed earlier. We need you to stay still. So, Leopold and Gunny are going to help you."

He saw them assembling a metal frame strapped to his head and anchored to the back of his chair. It was rudimentary and just two metal straps that closed in on each other and fastened with a wingnut. On the sides were two metal pieces that went from the sides to his shoulders, ending in an upside-down "U." It made Daniel think of crutches turned upside down. The doctor placed a blue sheet over his face and deftly cut out enough room for him to work. Meanwhile, Leopold and Gunny were strapping their arms to the chair. He felt a slight pinch in his arm.

"Sorry about that.", said Doc. "It's just a muscle relaxer. I don't need you jerking or flinching at the wrong time."

"No worries. Do what you have to do even if it doesn't work out. At least I know you tried."

"Thanks for the vote of confidence.", Doc said as he began the work earnestly. Daniels's mind drifted, and he heard Gunny talking to him. "Back when I was on leave in Bali before the war, I saw the sweetest piece of trim I have ever seen. She was a local girl. Brown skin, black wavy hair, full lips, and nice curves. She spoke English well enough, and all the boys loved her. But she only seemed to have an eye for officers."

The next thing he knew, they were finished, and he was helped into a wheelchair and deposited back in his bunk. Where he promptly fell asleep.

A few hours later, he awoke, and he felt that he had to go and check on his men. He found the ward and saw that most were in good spirits. Someone had found peanuts and cooked them up Southern Style by boiling them. This raised the men's morale. He felt hollow inside, as if he had survived the battle, but since he had lost his ship, he thought he had somehow failed the Navy and his family.

Charleston, South Carolina
November 1st, 1943

Two weeks had passed with no word, so Nimitz had arranged for Kim-Yee, Hailey, Jack, and Miranda to leave Hawaii bound for Charleston, SC. They spent two days flying and were utterly worn out when they arrived. Cars met them on the tarmac and were driven straight to the Core homestead. When they arrived, most of the clan was waiting for them. A large sign had been erected above the porch. It said, "Welcome Home, Family." Midora was there dressed in a dark dress with a grey apron, making a very imposing figure as she was almost six feet tall. Most of the family members were here today because it was Sunday. Only two of the males were present as they were underage for service. Daniels's father, Augustine, and Grandfather, Nikos, were still working the tugboat in the bay.

Kim-Yee looked out at the rather large assortment of people and steeled herself. She was dressed smartly in her Navy Whites, strode confidently up the steps, and introduced herself to Medora, who grabbed her in a bear hug with tears flowing freely. The eldest daughter, named Lyra, stepped in as her mother was crushing the breath out of Kim-Yee.

"Welcome to our home. I wish it were under better circumstances." she said, "Let's go inside."

Kim-Yee noted that the house was more prominent in the interior than it appeared outside as she entered. She wasn't sure if it was a trick of the light or just that there seemed to be mirrors everywhere. This house had a rather imposing history as it had been built by hand in the late 1800s and reflected that in its craftsmanship. It was a modest three-story home that had multiple rooms and two staircases. The plot was roughly an acre on the front and thirty at the rear. She could see crops growing, a vegetable garden on the right side, and a Martin garden on the left.

There is a rather long table with twenty seats, nine on each side and one at each end. It is dressed elaborately in linen and with fine china. There is a soup terrine and gravy boat. With all the trimmings, roasted beef, potatoes, carrots, baked ham, and turkey are laid out in a sumptuous feast. Midora urges Kim-Yee to sit at the seat of honor at the head. Her sister and children sit beside her. The rest of the family took their places and sat down, held hands, and prayed. Medora says, "Dear Heavenly Father, thank you for safely delivering our newest family members to our humble home. What's ours is theirs. We thank you for the food at the table even though we grew it, hunted it, killed it, and cooked it ourselves: thank you all the same. Please take care of our loved ones separated by this terrible world war and return them to us safely, healthy, hale, and hearty. Amen," There was a chorus of "Amen" from everyone at the table.

Kim-Yee smiled at the prayer, thinking, "I like this woman!"

There was a clatter as the food was passed around. They served the children first. She also noticed that the wine present was dark burgundy. Medora noticed her looking at it and said, "That is Elderberry wine. Jason, please pour your aunt a glass."

A lanky lad of twelve who resembled Daniel immensely stood and took the decanter in his hands, strode purposefully to her side, and expertly poured it, filling the glass halfway. Then, pleased he didn't spill a drop, he left it within arm's reach and returned to his seat.

Medora directed the conversation with Kim-Yee, introducing each family member, their age, and their contributions to the war effort. She could tell that it made her uncomfortable, and she decided to change the subject. "So, tell me, daughter. How did you meet my son?"

She told the tale, and everyone was spellbound.

She was staying at the Bachelors' Officers Quarters in Pearl Harbor at the base when she noticed a man dressed in a grey uniform entering the hotel. When he looked out the window, she called to him, saying," "Come on in the waters just fine."

He smiled and said, "Give me a minute." She was dressed in a modest two-piece with a flower in her hair and two Coca-Cola in hand. She handed him one and introduced herself. "Hi! I'm Kim-Yee."

He grinned and replied, "Daniel Core."

"Oh really?" she raised an eyebrow. "What? No rank? I saw you in a grey uniform. What does that mean?"

"It's a work uniform introduced to the Navy by Admiral King. It's not very popular as far as I can tell," he replied.

"Who gave you grief?" she asked.

"Admiral Jenkins.", he said.

"Whoa!" she replied.

"Yeah, I know," he said, sitting on a chaise lounge. "So, what brings you to Pearl?" he asked.

"No fair. Answer mine first. What's your rank?" she asked.

"Warrant Officer," he replied.

"Are you in charge of Clerks or a typing pool?" she asked.

"No, I was in charge of a destroyer until yesterday," he replied.

"Then you're a Captain?" she asked.

"Not yet; just a Warrant Officer; you can be a ship captain and not have the rank of Captain," he explained.

"Ah, yes. That's the Navy for you," she said. "How long will you be here for?" she asked.

"How about answer mine?" he said.

"That's fair. I'm just a nurse," she replied.

"No, you're not; you are an intricate cog in a huge machine," he explained. "I heard you laughing before I came out here. What was so funny?"

"A parrot flew in, and someone had trained it to curse in Cantonese."

"Well, that's different since Hong Kong is several thousand miles away. Did you teach it to talk that way?" he said half-mockingly.

"Why would you think it was me?"

"Because you are from Hong Kong."

"How did you know?"

"Accent mostly.", he replied, dead serious.

"What accent?"

"You have a slight British accent. Also, your sentence structure is very proper."

"Oh, come on. You can't get all of that from a sentence or two?"

"Can't I? Am I right?"

"Well, your case is strong, but what are some other giveaways?"

"How do you say the last letter of the English Alphabet?"

"E-Zed."

"See."

"No, I don't."

"We call it "Z.""

"Do you have any more examples?" she asked coyly.

He reached the table beside them and grabbed a small notepad and golf pencil. He wrote something down. "Pronounce this word.", he instructed.

"Aluminum."

He smirked," We call it Aluminum."

"Okay, you win. That's a very talented set of ears that you have."

They continued chatting about nothing, trying to avoid discussing the war and its horrors. She finally asked him, "What are your plans for dinner?"

"I was just going to drop by the Chow Hall," he said.

"Nah! Let's go out to someplace local, "she said frankly.

"Sure. But I think it's too late to sign out a Jeep from the motor pool, and I just landed. Let me get over to disbursement and grab my pay," he said.

"Don't worry about it. My uncle has a Chinese Restaurant off base. We can eat there. I'll get ready. Meet out front in an hour?"

Hailey remarked, "Wow! You never told me about that."

She continued, "So I introduced him to Dim Chinese breakfast" and told them all about the dishes and flavors, and they were intrigued.

"You will have to show me how to make some of that.", said Midora.

"Well, we will need certain ingredients that I don't think you have on hand," she began.

"Dear lady, this is a seaport. If it came on a ship, it could be had. Make a list; we shall obtain the items.", said Medora with a finality that impressed her. But then again, with sixteen people under one roof, she guessed that she had to be stern to keep everyone in line.

Later that afternoon, all the items had been bought and assembled in the kitchen. Kim-Yee and Hailey showed Medora and Kim how to trim the fat off the pork roast and then cover it with a red paste. "Now we cook it in a pan over a low and steady heat for several hours. Then we pull it out in the last fifteen minutes and slather it with honey." All nodded.

While the pork was cooking, Kim-Yee showed them how to prepare the rice flour to make bao. "So, we make the dough and let it rise. Then, once the Barbeque Pork is ready, we will chop it up and season it with onion, salt, ginger, and Hoisin sauce. This will be the filling. Then we roll the dough out flat into little disks, take the filling, and drop it into the middle. Then, tuck the sides up and pinch it off. Next, we placed it in the steamer and waited about fifteen minutes." She also demonstrated how to make dumplings, which was the same process as the bao but with a different kind of covering. This was an egg noodle type that had been rolled flat and cut into squares.

"That looks like a smaller version of an empanada.", said Medora.

"Yes, I've heard that before but never had one.", remarked Kim-Yee as she fried up half of the dumplings.

"Yes, those were my son Darian's favorite."

"Wait a second. Who's Darian?"

"Your husband."

"You mean Danny?"

Medora started laughing, full-on-throat, which brought tears to her eyes. "Yes. The same."

"I'm confused."

Lyra spoke up as she saw her mother gasping for breath. "My brother's full name is Darian Christos Corenaphenos. On his first day of school, the teachers decided that since they already had a student named Dorian, his name would be too confusing. So, they gave him the name Daniel. Which comes with the nickname Danny."

Hailey piped up, "But your last name is Core?"

60

Medora picked up the story, "When my husband's father came to this country and immigrated through Ellis Island, he told them his full name. But the typewriter ribbon ran out of ink. Therefore, it only caught the first four letters of our name. He figured new country, a new name. It seems to be a theme here."

Kim-Yee smirked at that, then returned to business as she assembled the ingredients to make the shui-mai. "We take the water chestnuts and dice them up. Then, take the cooked shrimp and do likewise. Next, add a few dashes of seasoning and some diced green onions, and we take the same skins from the dumplings, but take the spoon and use your hand to bring up the sides and twist it a little."

"That looks like a Mallow cup.", said Lyra.

"Then these get steamed as well."

Next came the greens. Kim-Yee instructed them, "Make sure to rinse these in salt water as they might have a few hangers on."

"Like what?" asked Lyra.

"How about this little critter," said Hailey as she picked a snail up from the water.

"Yes, but there might also be sand, dirt, and slugs. Rinse everything at least three times or until the water is clear without any sediment at the bottom of the bowl. Clear glass is the best; you can see what's coming from the vegetables.

A few hours later, the table was set again, with a delectable spread of Chinese Food. There was Chinese Barbeque pork, dumplings, Shu-mei, and Char-Siu Bao. For the vegetables, they prepared Chinese Broccoli and Napa cabbage. Both had been steamed and flavored with soy sauce, sesame, peanut oil, and Hoisin, then a large pot of white rice to accompany it all.

The families' eyes were wide as they surveyed the meal. Then, they all sat down for this light snack. Hailey and Jack showed their cousins how to use chopsticks. Most were slightly clumsy but got the hang of it after a few minutes. There was laughter as they tried, and a few casualties dropped onto the table but were quickly scooped up by hands and popped into mouths. This family lived by the motto of waste, not want, not.

Medora surveyed her family's new members and noticed her daughter-in-law's sadness. Oh, she put up a good front but could tell that maybe she was finally coming to terms with Darian's disappearance and possible death. She could tell he profoundly affected this woman and her children and was glad of it. Her son was full of love; even if he had only been in their lives for a bit, they would forever love him, which was good enough for her.

The Nightmares

Daniel was asleep, and his mind was adrift. He remembered being at the tail end of the convoy. He and his men were all at their action stations; they had done enough drills and worked together so long that all their movements were in concert. The Patrol Craft was a 173-foot-long, 450-ton diesel engine with a single 3-inch gun open to the elements on deck, depth charges, anti-submarine rocket launchers, a 40mm cannon, and three double-barreled autocannons. In essence, it resembled a smaller version of a destroyer. Its typical job consisted of convoy escort and anti-submarine warfare.

Daniel was on the bridge with Mr. Cureton, the executive officer, as he was striking for the position. As he was busy signing reports and seeing to the business of running the ship with all men at their posts, a watcher called out. "Kate's and Zeroes on approach eleven o clock." Kate's were bombers, and Zeroes were fighters.

"Helm comes to heading 271.", said Daniel.

"271 Aye, sir.", said the helmsman as he adjusted the course. He was dressed in a Navy work uniform and wore a soft collar chambray shirt with bell-bottom dungaree material pants, a navy-blue knitted belt, and a white cover.

"All stations report manned and ready! Here they come! Target Aircraft sighted bearing one eight zero position angle two five," said Waisner, and they all heard the distinct sound of Zero's engine. It had a high-pitched whine, turning into a deep rumble and roar as it flew overhead with the pinging of lead as they strafed the ship.

"Barrage Fire! Take dive attack sectors!" Daniel called out in a crisp and steady voice. His men shot back rapid fire using a pre-calculated fixed range, and the guns elevated sixty degrees so that when a target continued its course at the same speed, they would pass right through it. These devastating interlocking fields of fire they had established made short work of the Zeros and downed several enemy planes within a minute. Their main job was to run interference and protect the larger ships in the convoy. Be it from airplanes, other ships, or submarines. They were the tip of the spear.

The Zeroes swarmed in from all angles; over 100 fired their guns and swept the convoy with hot lead. These fighters were speedy but had a vulnerability in their fuel tanks. If his men could target the sweet spot, they could down the planes quickly. Sometimes it was a matter of skill, and sometimes it was luck. Either it was with you or the pilot.

They were busy protecting this small flotilla at Bokak Atoll. "PORT SIDE TORPEDO BOMBER!" called a watchstander excitedly. He turned and saw the plane coming in under his guns about forty feet above the water.

"HELM HARD LEEWARD!" yelled Daniel.

"HARD LEEWARD AYE!" the helmsman said as he frantically spun the wheel to the left.

"Come on, come on, come ON! ALL GUNS FIRE LOCALLY!! Direct fire to match parallax." Daniel said. "Rapid continuous fire!"

The ship groaned and turned to the left, leaning upwards at about a 15-degree pitch. It was enough to give the gunners the correct angle to hit the aircraft, and it exploded. They might have hit the gas tank or the torpedo. But they didn't have time to think about it as planes came in from every angle. Daniel saw another plane go down, and its ruptured gas tank spewed a lethal arc of combustible fuel everywhere. The Japs had enough planes through the screen and were targeting the carriers. Another dive bomber climbed to 1500 feet and started its run when a 30mm gun mount from another Patrol Craft took it out.

Unfortunately, as the plane broke up into pieces, the engine struck amidships, killing many men. But the support ship had effectively screened the carrier.

He saw a 500-pound bomb hit a destroyer and slam into the rudder; now, they couldn't steer. He was too far away to help and too busy to fall out of position in the order of battle.

He awoke bathed in sweat, wearing just his skivvies and a t-shirt. He could hear Marines pounding on the door to his cabin. "SIR? Are you all right?"

He rolled out of bed and staggered to the door; as he arrived, it was wrenched open. Two Marines had their pistols raised. One grabbed him and pulled him out of the cabin, and the other swept in and, after a few seconds, yelled, "CLEAR!"

He was bewildered. "Why are you here?" he asked.

"Because you were screaming, sir." the marine guard told him bluntly. A doctor came down the corridor with a metal syringe. He walked up to Daniel with a sad look in his eyes as he jabbed him in the shoulder and hit the plunger. "This should help you to get some sleep." Daniel was steered towards his bunk, and he fell to one side. The doctor pocketed the syringe and helped to cover him up. He could hear them talking but barely made out what they were saying.

"Is he going to be all right, Doc?"

"Maybe, but he just underwent the major trauma of losing his ship and half his men. He is shell-shocked. He might recover but needs to heal at a decent-sized hospital with the right facilities."

He awoke to find himself in the hospital ward among the officers. Some had it worse than he did; many were missing limbs, and their bodies were torn up. Most of the casualties were from the recent battle in the area. Some of them had been blinded, and he noticed one had a stack of mail, so he got up, went over to his bed, and asked his name.

"Anderson," came the reply.

"I'm Daniel Core. If you want, I can read this mail here for you."

"That would be swell. Thanks."

So, he opened the first letter and read it to his wounded companion. He had difficulty concentrating on the words, and his focus went in and out. Several hours later, the entire stack of mail had been read through, and Anderson had drifted off to sleep.

He went to the officer's mess, and to his amazement, they were serving ham steaks with lima beans. There was bread with real pats of butter and a bowl of pickles. Canned peaches and ice cream were for dessert. There was coffee with natural sugar and rich, heavy cream. He appreciated every bite. He talked to the other officers from the battle, and they shared their individual stories.

Burt was from the USS Helena, a Brooklyn class light cruiser. She had fought in the Battles of Cape Esperance, Guadalcanal, and Kula Gulf. She was the first ship to receive the Navy Unit Commendation. He could talk endlessly about his boat, which helped to pass the time.

"So, how long was your ship?" Daniel asked.

"608 feet long and displaced 12,207 long tons at full displacement. We had two catapults on the fantail that could launch four Curtis SOC Seagull floatplanes, which are great for aerial surveillance."

"How many boilers did you have?"

"Eight Babcock & Wilcox boilers drove the four Parsons steam turbines."

"What was your crew compliment?"

"888- 52 officers and 836 enlisted. How about yourself?"

"I ran a Patrol Craft. I had a single pop 3" cannon but multiple antiaircraft and Bofors Guns. I also had an excellent hedgehog mortar launching system. I even used it once firing high on a light cruiser, and it rent the forecastle."

"Not a bad tactic. Your little ships can gang up on larger vessels and tear them a new one. Most people don't think to give you enough credit."

"I know we are just the destroyer escorts. But we can get into the shallows and go where others can't."

"Maybe one day you'll write a book about it?"

"First, I have to survive the war."

There was a pilot seated named Barnwell. He spoke up about his exploits. "I was a pilot in a B-52 Bomber, and we were dispatched to blow up a bridge near a Japanese base. Of course, we had no escort and encountered heavy resistance from the Zeros. They shredded us up quickly, and we all had to bail out. We, those damn Japs decided to strafe us on the way down. So, I just hung limp. I planned to play possum until they were right on me. It worked. One of them slowed down to get a good look at me, and that's when I pulled my 1911 from my leg pouch and fired four shots directly into the canopy. I hit the pilot, and he careened out of control and crashed."

"That's an amazing tale.", said Burt.

"It's the truth."

"Well, good for you," said Daniel.

Waisner spoke up, "Once we were doing "unrest" (underway replenishment) with several ships in a task force. We were going about 5-7 knots and the ship we were going to send munitions to pulled up alongside us and matched speed. I heard my name called over the speakers, and they announced that I was to 'lay into the armory' as it was my turn to shoot the throwing line to the other ship. I get to the armory and am handed an M1 with the attachment and five blanks. The ship was about 100 yards away, and the winds were about twenty-five knots. The Master of Arms asked me if I'd ever done this before. I told him, 'Nope.' Just fire your counterpart over there. By the way, I bet you $5; you can't hit it. I ask to see the cash, and he pulls it out and shows it to me. So, I fired it and got it in one. Easiest five bucks I've ever made."

Home to Roost
November 15th, 1943

Several days later, they docked, and he was put on a bus and driven to the main hospital. He knew this was a routine procedure, but he didn't like it. He spent a few days in quarantine, where they checked on his eye and saw that it was improving, and the swelling had gone down tremendously. He struggled to know from it; his vision was like looking through cotton. After a few days, he was told to report to Command for a hearing on losing his ship.

He arrived on time, and he could tell that it was a formality as the records and accounts were read by all parties present and recorded. The whole process took several hours, and they adjourned for lunch. Two hours later, the inquest resumed, and he was acquitted.

Then, he was escorted to the runway and put on a flight. He landed in San Francisco and was whisked away on another flight over land. He flew to Midlands, Texas, and then to Belle Chase, Louisiana. He was transferred to another plane and finally arrived in Charleston, SC. Bewildered, he was driven to the main headquarters building, where he was given a cursory physical and orders to report to command the following day. He was billeted in the bachelor's officers' quarters or the BOQ, a hotel for the officers in transit or on short-stay duty.

He arrived promptly at the appointed time and was told he would be put in charge of a training cadre for officers assuming command of Patrol Craft and Destroyer Escort ships. He was also asked if he wanted to join his family as they were on base already, and he had a few days before the training started.

"I thought they were in Hawaii."

"No. They were transferred here a few weeks back."

"That's why no one picked up when I tried to call."

Then it hit him that Nimitz had planned this for them, and there were tears in his eyes. "What is the address?"

"7 Windward Way."

"Get out of here."

"No, seriously. Why?"

"Because my address at Pearl was 234 Windward Way."

"I guess it's just one of those street names that every city has. Like Fairview Lane."

"Yeah, that's probably it."

He left Admin and walked the two blocks to the motor pool, where he attempted to check out a Wiley Jeep, but they refused because of his eye patch. So, one of the men drove to the address. He looked at the little yellow bungalow on a breezy corner and got choked up as it looked just like their little house in Hawaii. He saw all of his family's shoes lined up at the front door and smelled the wonderful aroma of the Asian cooking that he had become accustomed to. He opened the screen door and called out. "Hey, Sis! What's cooking?"

Miranda, his sister-in-law, turned around and dropped her cup of tea. Luckily, it happened to be a tin mug. She swooned, and he ran to get her before she hit the floor.

"Aya, you're supposed to be dead."

He helped get her to a chair, and she put her head between her knees until she could get enough oxygen. Then she looked up at him and grinned from ear to ear.

"Sis Eight will not believe me when I tell her she was right. You are just missing, not dead."

"Where is Kim-Yee?"

"At the clinic."

"Clinic?"

"Yes, she is on midwife rotation, and because of the full moon, women have been dropping babies left and right."

"How are the children?"

"Coping, but sad."

"As Mark Twain said, 'The news of my death has been greatly exaggerated.' I sent word that I was all right, but I missed you as you were already in transit, and so was I."

Miranda put the vegetables, herbs, and spices in the icebox, cut the stove off, and grabbed the keys.

He got in the War Wagon, and she drove them to the clinic. He didn't care about anything else. He just had to see his wife. As they pulled up to the building, he could see that the clinic was full, but he strode past everyone and into the bowels of the facility. He went straight to the ward section, where he would probably run into her. As he came around a corner to ask her whereabouts, he heard a rattle and crash as a pan was dropped. He looked straight at her and ran to envelop her in his arms. She could hardly breathe, and her voice was tiny. "You came back."

"I told you I would.", he said.

She wept joyfully, and the head nurse motioned for her to go. They left the building arm in arm. She was giddy but also was fighting to breathe as her emotions overwhelmed her.

They went to the school to pick up the children. They marched to the building and checked them out. Both were escorted and when they saw him, they ran, crying, "DADDY!". Hailey hugged him, fiercely crying, and Jack was jumping around, trying to get in a hug. Then, finally, he gave up and folded his arms around Daniels's waist.

They drove to the Officer's Club for dinner. He let them talk and talk and talk about what had happened in the time that they had been separated. He said very little about his exploits, just giving noncommittal evasive answers.

Jack asked, "Daddy, what happened to your face?"

"I slipped and fell on the ship and went for a swim."

Hailey changed subjects quickly and told him about the prank war that had started between her and Jack.

"Really? Tell me more.", he said.

Hailey began, "It all started when Jill, Mickey, and I hosted a party, and a few boys came over.

"With permission, I gather. Who are Jill and Mickey?"

"My best friends"

Kim-Yee said," Oh yes, the whole thing was approved and chaperoned."

"This little stinker decided it would be a good idea to use those snap bag poppers at us during the dance."

"I bet that went over well."

"Yeah. It caused the party to be broken up."

"So, you retaliated."

"Yeah, I got him back."

"How?"

"I put salt in the sugar bowl."

Daniel looked at Jack and asked, "How did you get her back?"

He looked around sheepishly and said, "I put a rubber snake in her panty drawer."

Hailey busted out laughing, "That was a good one."

Kim-Yee broke in, "Then she put dish powder in the sugar bowl, and he looked like a mad dog."

Hailey said, "It all came to a head when he figured out a way to sneak Mentos into the top of the Coke bottles."

Daniel asked, "What happens then?"

"Once you open the top, the candy falls into the bottle, creating a lava foam that starts boiling out."

Kim-Yee spoke up, "That's when I stopped the prank war. Because of the force of that, Mentos and Coke could take an eye out. I told them I would whip them both the next time there was a prank."

Jack looked sheepishly at his dad, "Am I in trouble?"

Daniel replied, smiling. "No, son. It sounds like your mother handled it."

They spent the rest of the time catching up. He listened to their stories and didn't say anything about his ordeal.

The chef rolled a cart out for them, removing the large silver cover with a flourish. "Voila, Peeking Duck."

The rich smell of aromatic herbs hit them. They surveyed the roasted crispy duck skin, the white flat disks of bao, the barbeque smell of the hoisin sauce, and the smells of freshly chopped ginger and green onions. The chef expertly carved the duck breast into perfectly cut slices, which he placed on the bao, added a little bit of the rest, and served one each to them. Then, while they were eating, he hacked the duck into its pieces and turned and left.

"So, how is school?" asked Daniel as he folded the bao and bit into it.

"Why do you ask?" asked Hailey.

"New schools require adjustments. Sometimes it's not easy. Just wondering."

"Well...now that you mention it. The first day was a little awkward."

"How?"

"Well, the teacher asked me to come to the front of the class and introduce myself. I did, and this link asked me why my name sounded so normal."

"What do you mean?" Daniel asked.

His name was Lonnie, and he said, "Well, most of your people's names sound like you threw a pie plate out into the street.", as he snickered.

"So, what did you do?" Daniel asked.

"I handled it as I marched over to the blackboard and wrote 'Kim-Yee.'

That's my mother's name, and in traditional Chinese naming conventions, I have to be named something that rhymes or matches it. So, the name chosen for me was Hailey. This defines my place and position in the family line. Unlike you, who has to say this, my cousin Earl from my mother's side. In Chinese culture, the name gives your rank."

"How about you, Jack?"

"Schools fine, I guess," he replied noncommittally.

They enjoyed the remainder of the duck and had the rest packed to go. Daniel signed the check and thanked the chef personally. Then, they all piled into the car and drove home. It was getting dark, and the family started its turning-in routine. He took a shower and felt the swelling around his eye. He could feel everyone trying not to look at it. Luckily, the trip back had taken a few weeks, and his hair had mainly grown since, which hid many of the scars. But looking in the mirror, he could see that his left eyelid had been stitched up the middle. He shrugged and thought, 'I'm still here. A little worse for wear, but still here.' He exited the bathroom, went to the master bedroom, and donned pajamas. He wore a bathrobe and looked up at the stars outside. He was sitting out on the veranda, feeling the cool breezes. Hailey came up and sat down beside him.

"Dad?" Hailey asked.

"Yes, dear."

"Why are you so quiet?"

"I don't know. Am I?"

"Yes, you are, and that's not like you."

"Well, I had a tough time out there. I lost my ship and half of my men. I'm surprised I'm still an officer."

"Well, that's war. You did your job and trained your men well. They loved serving under you and would do anything for you. Don't be so hard on yourself."

"Since when did you get so wise?"

"When you weren't looking."

"What's up, sport?"

"What do you mean?"

"You want to talk about something."

"I do. Remember me telling you about the Subbayas?"

"Yes, the elderly Japanese couple that lived across the street from your old place. He was a gardener, and they had a granddaughter about your age. Her name was Sumire?"

"Yes."

"What about them?"

"They were swept up in the raids and are in Honouliuli Internment camp on Oahu."

"That's rather unfortunate.", he said warily.

"I know. It's not right. They are living in a 20x20 room made from plywood and tar paper. The conditions are barely sanitary."

"How do you know this?"

"Because I have been in contact with Sumire and was there when they were taken."

"How did it happen?"

"The FBI showed up early in the morning and started tossing the place, looking for short wave radios, cameras, anything they could confiscate, and I heard the screaming and crying. So, I grabbed my pass, put on a robe, and went there. The policemen stopped me, and another told him to toss me into the truck. I held out my pass and showed him I was Chinese and an American. He told me to wait for one and brought out Sumire, who was hysterically crying. 'Calm her down.' But don't go far.

So, we returned across the street, sat on the stoop, and Auntie made her some tea. She was shaking uncontrollably.

"That must have been very traumatic. But that was several years ago. Why are you bringing it up now?"

"Because we've been writing to each other, Mr. Subbaya has died, and Mrs. Subbaya is in a coma. She has no one."

"Ok. That's a problem."

"The only reason they were being held is that they are Issei (Japanese-born people who are not eligible for citizenship), but Sumire isn't. She's an American and should be granted all rights!"

"Whoa, Slow down their sport. I'm not the enemy."

"No, but the military is. Hawaii is under martial law, and whatever the military says goes. The people there have no rights."

"What do you want from me?"

"I want her to get out of that camp."

"Then what?"

"Then come here to live with us."

"That's a big ask."

"Just read the letters," she said as she produced a bundle, handed it to him, and then strode back into the house.

"Wow!", just like her mother.", he said to himself as he sat down and read them.

To: Hailey Chung From Sumire Subbaya

#234 Windward Way Sand Island Internment Camp

Pearl Harbor, Hawaii Oahu, Hawaii

December 10th, 1941

Hailey,

I want to thank you for the kindness you showed me and my grandparents on that awful day when those men from the government came and took us away. We were only allowed to take with us what we could carry. Grandfather put everything he could manage into a large bundle from a quilt and strapped it to his back. Grandmother was worried and tried to take tea and rice, but these were slammed out of her hands and dashed to the floor. They said, 'That's not necessarily where you're going.' He said it in such a cruel way she thought they were taking us to be executed for the crime of being Japanese. She knelt in supplication and bared her throat, expecting to be killed on the spot. He thought she was crazy and had her hauled out to the waiting truck. She was meek and timid, with all signs of resignation. Then they came for me and tore me from the loving arms of your family. I will never forget the look of horror on your face as we were driven off to who knows where.

They stopped several times and picked up more and more people until the truck was full. Then they drove us to a camp. It had barbed wire fences and guard towers. We were all herded out of the trucks and lined up before the center. Two administrators from the War Relocation Authority sat at a table and quickly proceeded to check us in.

We all had to report to the hospital next for health checkups, then to the group showers. After which, we were given housing and some bedding.

They put us in tents, saying the barracks would be built in a few weeks. The Commandant saw Grandfather working with his hands, creating a table and chairs out of scrap wood, and gave him a job doing repairs around the camp for $16 a month. Grandmother and I both work in the kitchens for $12 a month.

Most of the food here comes from cans and tastes very bland and industrial. In the morning, we are served tea, then lunch consists of a thin soup with soggy potatoes, and dinner is a piece of bread and a slice of Vienna sausage. This dinner was also supposed to supplement our breakfast.

The work in the kitchen is hard because the stoves run on coal, and it's very depressing. There are no fresh fruits or vegetables. So, the men decided to send off seeds and asked for plots to cultivate.

I'll write back as soon as I can.

Your friend for life

Sumire

From: Hailey Chung To: Sumire Subbaya

#234 Windward Way Sand Island Internment Camp

Pearl Harbor, Hawaii Oahu, Hawaii

December 29, 1941

Dear Sumire,

That could sound better. I will send you some school supplies and seeds as soon as possible. I was walking down the streets and saw many abandoned and shuttered businesses. I got a lot of strange looks from people and was stopped three times by military police who demanded to see my papers and wanted to know why I wasn't in a camp. I told them that I was born here and am Chinese.

Hailey

He stared at the lengthy correspondence and wondered how she had both parts of the letters. Then, it dawned on him that she made copies to have a record in case she needed proof that she was contacting or attempting to correspond with her friend.

To: Hailey Chung From Sumire Subbaya

January 5th, 1942

Thank you for the seeds and pencils in the case. The can of rice pudding was also appreciated. I hate to ask you, but my grandfather told me that when your mother entered military service, she had signed a piece of paperwork that made them godparents for you and your brother Jack. Would that document help me out in the event of their deaths?

The school has started, but there is no schoolhouse, so we have to hold it in the cafeteria. We also have no supplies; the teachers are all Caucasian, and they do not allow us to speak our native language.

Life here is boring: eat, sleep, school, work, eat, sleep.

Sumire

From: Hailey Chung To: Sumire Subbaya

March 12th, 1942

Dear Sumire,

I hope you are doing well. It's lonely here without my Mother. She is away a lot, helping out as a Nurse. I'm enclosing part of my allowance, and several mail-order catalogs. I've also held a piece of indigo. You can use it to dye clothing. I forgot to tell you that my Mom remarried. It came as quite a shock to us. She met him before we got to the house at Pearl. He is white and an officer who served in the Orient for two years before the war broke out. He is good to us and treats us like his own.

Hailey

To: Hailey Chung From Sumire Subbaya

#234 Windward Way Honouliuli Internment Camp

Pearl Harbor, Hawaii Oahu, Hawaii

April 1st, 1943

Dear Hailey,

They moved us to a different camp, as Sand Island was temporary. The buildings were all slapped together quickly with no thought about quality. The first thing Grandfather did was to remove all the nails and reposition the wood. He was making it as plumb as he could. But that still left a gap at the top, so he searched around, came up with some apple crates, and used the reclaimed wood to make the remainder of the wall. He was very resourceful and made a table and folding chairs, then created beds for us.

Thank you very much for the gifts. Our rations have improved, and they have started incorporating rice into our diet. Today, we made a cut-up hot dog dish with powdered eggs over rice. It's not the best but better than those soggy canned potatoes.

The men in the camp have been working hard on the schoolhouse. It should be ready in a few days. The local library has donated many discarded books for us to use.

The Army came and asked for volunteers for an all-Nisei Regiment. Several young men came forward and left for training. Could you come and visit sometime?

Sumire

From: Hailey Chung To: Sumire Subbaya

April 11, 1943

I tried to visit but was turned away at a checkpoint a few miles away. They told me I would not be allowed to leave if I went to the camp. For "Operational Security."

They detained me for questioning for several hours and verified that all of my documents were real. Finally, they drove me home with a stern warning that they would keep me next time. I will try to get the word out about your plight. Keep the letters coming.

Your sister

Hailey

To: Hailey Chung From Sumire Subbaya

May 1st, 1943

Hey Sis,

Understand that they are reading the mail, and I can't tell you everything. Most things that I want to write would be censored. We got a hold of some sweet rice and a bit of Nori (seaweed), so we fried up some spam and made Spam sushi. We aren't starving here, but the food is very dull. We try to come up with various ways to liven it up. So, we made up a dish called Shoyu Weenies, where we cut the hot dogs into slices, stir fry some onions, added sugar and soy sauce, and served it over rice.

Ja' ne,

Sumire

He was not sure what he could do, if anything. However, Sumire said something in one of her first letters about them being godparents for Hailey and Jack. He wondered about the legalities and how to work that. He knew all the documents, wills, and records were transferred to his aegis when he married her mother. Now, it was his problem. He went to Hailey's room, and she sat in bed, eagerly awaiting a response. "Hailey, let me ask you a question. When we first met, you challenged authority and declared yourself an American. Is this what all of that stemmed from?"

She looked down sheepishly and replied, "Yes, Dad."

"Why did it take you so long to come to me with this?"

"I don't know. I thought if I asked you for help, then it might appear as if I was being un-American. They were declared enemy aliens. But she shouldn't even be there. Can't you help...in some way?"

"I will go in and talk to some lawyers first thing tomorrow. I have a little bit of time before the training cadre starts. No promises. But I will try to do something."

She surged forward into his arms and hugged him tightly, "Thanks, Dad! I knew that I could count on you."

He kissed her on the top of her head, got up, and left, closing the door behind him. He entered the kitchen, where his wife was heating milk on the stove. "What was all that about?"

"Hailey asked me to look into the plight of your neighbors, the Subbayas."

"The children's godparents?"

"Yes. How did that happen?"

"Well, when I volunteered for Officer training, I needed at least two separate entities to take over if I was killed or disabled in the line of duty. Miranda, of course, was one, and the Subbayas were the other. It made sense because they had helped us in the past looking after the children since their granddaughter was around Hailey's age. I also wanted to give them some legitimacy on paper and keep them from being swept up in the raids. It bought them some time but not enough, as they were taken anyway. What gives?"

"Mr. Subbaya has died, and Mrs. Subbaya is in a coma from a broken heart. Sumire is alone, and Hailey wants me to try to get her out since she is Nisei. There is no reason for them to keep her any longer."

"Okay, well then, go and take care of it. They were good to the children, and we must be good back to them."

"I will say first thing in the morning."

He got into bed with his wife and slept without dreaming for the first time in a long while.

True to his word, the next day, he went in to inquire about Sumire, filled out several forms, and met with various administration staff who assured him they would look into it and get back to him shortly.

He didn't think much of it and went to the base school to meet with the Principal about his children's grades and deportment. He was assured that the staff knew his children were Chinese, and they didn't see any problems or anticipate any.

Then, the training started, and he got busy with the routine. The doctors were still concerned about his left eye. It wasn't tracking as well as they had hoped. He put up with their poking, prodding, and prescriptions, but one day, he had enough and said, "Look, Doc. I know you mean well, but you have to understand that I got hit right above the eye by a machine gun bullet. I'm lucky to be still able to see. Maybe 70-80% vision is all I will get from now on. Time will tell. But I'm lucky to be alive and still here, in one piece, more or less. I'll take that. But I'm leaving and won't be back unless I notice some green puss oozing out of the whites of my eyes or my whole face slack. Capiche?"

The Ophthalmologist nodded in agreement. "Okay. But if I see you around the base and it doesn't look good, I'll grab you by the arm and quickly march you to my chair. Deal?"

"Deal!"

He got up and went back to the training area. He was thinking about when he had finished OCS and was sent to training in Pearl, how the officer in charge, Captain Garrison, had started the training classes so nonchalantly. Now, it was his turn. Luckily, the training regimen had several guest speakers, and they were lined up. His main job was to train the men taking over the Patrol Craft. The course materials consisted of the following books: Naval Tactics and Coastal Defense, Fleet Tactics and Naval Operations, Fleet Tactics Theory and Practice, Examples, Conclusions, and Maxims of Modern Naval Tactics.

The outline for the class consisted of nine pillars:
Ships Organization
Engineering

Gunnery
Sound Gear Techniques
Attack doctrine and tactics
Escort- Patrol- Ship Handling
Ship Maintenance
Qualifications of the Naval Officer, by John Paul Jones
The Laws of the Navy by Captain Hopwood, R.N.
He looked at the schedule. It was reasonable. Mostly 09:00-17:00
Monday through Wednesday, with Thursday and Friday set for
'Practical Practice' and Saturday as optional weather makeup.

Combat & Tactics Training

Daniel stood in the classroom and looked at the fifty men assembled, "Good morning. I am your instructor for the course. It will be on Naval Combat and Tactics. You are obviously in the wrong room if that information is new. Please correct that error." He paused, said, "Great," and then walked over and locked the door. "We have a lot of ground to cover. But first, we need to get introductions out of the way. So, I want each one of you to stand up. State your name and rank, followed by your length of service and what type of vessel you served on." They each took their turn. Once introductions were completed, he carried on. "The military relies on data. Information can change over time. Sometimes, it's a simple mistake to take down the information firsthand. Other times, it's when it's entered into the record or translated into another format or language. People don't know what you meant. They only know what you wrote. So, when you write your reports, always keep the tone correct and your comments brief and to the point. This will be a master's class in the subject, and the information here is classified as "Secret." You will review data as close to real-time as we can manage. For starters, we will be discussing naval formations and the latest battle doctrine. We will be covering naval battles from 1090 to 1914 in the text. Real-world events will supplement the rest. Brace yourselves; this will be a bumpy ride. We will have class Monday-Wednesday. It will be from 08:00-17:00. There will be a lunch break around noon for one hour and two bathroom breaks as needed. On Thursday and Friday, we will have wet classes on various vessels. Saturday will be a makeup day. Sunday will be off for a day of rest and Divine Services. You are expected to be prompt, and I need your undivided attention. We will go very fast, and you will need to keep up. There will also be 30 pages of reading per text per day. Does everyone get that?"

"Aye, sir!" came the chorus from the students.

"Good, then let's begin. Our first foray into the topic will be the Battle of the Koyun Islands. Does anyone have any input? You their third row. " He quickly scanned the roster and zeroed in on a Greek student. "Mr. Apropos."

"I'm sorry to say, sir. I've never heard of this one," the student replied sheepishly.

"Well, that might be because it happened in 1090AD during the Byzantine Empire. But it was a remarkable feat by someone outclassed and overwhelmed yet still managed to stomp his opponent... So, what are the best things to have to your advantage in a naval engagement?" The class went on, and he followed the curriculum without fail. Some students easily get the material, and some still need to. The real challenge was to see how all of the aspects of the classroom applied to the actual training on the various classes of ships they might end up commanding. The next thing he knew, it was time for lunch, but since they were on an accelerated schedule, they would not break for lunch. Boxed lunches and drinks were brought in, and they continued. "A central concept in modern naval fleet warfare is the battlespace: a zone around the flotilla where each ship performs its duties correctly. The purpose of the PT boats is to screen the task force and attack targets at the direction of the Commodore or Admiral. The Minesweeper is there to detect and engage threats before they become dangerous to the convoy. The destroyer is there to screen the larger ships like battleships and aircraft carriers. The cruisers are there to run down detected enemies and support the larger vessels. The battlecruiser is the last line of defense in this arrangement. Of course, all this works in concert to see the enemy without being detected. Therefore, submarines and aircraft are also included in the detection bubble. Open water is the best location for a fleet as the land's topography can help the enemy determine precisely where a fleet might anchor and place itself in a field of Naval Battle since the draft of each type of ship is known.

Also, these ships are essential to protect the various other support vessels like oilers, colliers, tankers, tenders, ammunition, rescue, and hospital ships," he droned on. Then, it was time for the class to end, and everyone went home.

They were back at it the next day, and he had everything set up in a War Room where they had many visual aids. The guest lecturer was Major Garrison—the man who had trained him. There was a large table that had a topographical map on it. It was over 30 feet across and 10 feet deep. There were little models set up that could be moved around the board with long sticks. He thought back to his first battle, which now was the doctrine of what not to do. Major Garrison began the lecture, " Remember that the orders will come from the Commodore, and if you had information that would cause a conflict in those orders, make sure to relay that to him because you may have a different line of sight. But the decision is theirs. You must follow orders. Period. Especially in a time of war, your job is to gather information and relay said report so they can make better-informed decisions. Take the Battle of the Java Sea that transpired at the beginning of the war. It was referred to as ABDACOM, an acronym for American-British-Dutch Australian Command. Three main problems crippled this command.

First, they integrated sailors from four countries and three different navies who spoke other languages. Secondly, they needed more airpower, which hampers intelligence gathering. Thirdly, any mechanical breakdowns meant that if they could retire for repairs, it would be Surabaya, the main target for air attacks by the Japanese, or the floating dry-dock at Tjiltap, which is on the southern coast. If the ships were severely injured, they were to be scuttled. The defense force for the area only consisted of fourteen warships. There was Strike Force 10 for the immediate defense, which consisted of the heavy cruisers HMS Exeter and USS Houston; light cruisers Hr. De Ruyter, Hr. Ms. Java and HMAS Perth; and destroyers HMS Electra, HMS Encounter, HMS Jupiter, Hr. MS. Korteaner, Hr.MS Witt de With, USS John D. Edwards, USS Alden, USS John Ford, and USS John Paul Jones."

A voice said, "Major, why is an Army officer teaching the course?"

"Oh, that's easy because the Corps of Discovery helped to map the rivers and coastal waterways that the Corps of Engineers took over. We also have boats. Any more questions?" he waited a moment, and the lecture continued, "Spotter aircraft was low on fuel when it caught sight of 56 troop means of transport headed to the west of Java with warship escorts, and 41 means of transport were sent to the eastern end. Admiral Doorman was ordered to 'Attack the enemy until they are destroyed.' The hope was to send the meager defense force to meet and take out the Japanese convoy, return to base, and then rearm and sortie out again to pound the second convoy. Admiral Doorman went out to sweep for these attackers but could not find them after two days of searching. His superior was angered at his lack of results, and his reply was, 'Let me know where they are, and I will engage them!' Unfortunately, the crews were at the point of exhaustion as they had been at Battle Stations almost nonstop for two days, so he decided to return to base, and he was spotted by Japanese Aircraft when he made his about-face turn.

When the defenders were attacked, they wandered into a minefield. They engaged two destroyer flotillas, six destroyers under the command of Rear Admiral Nishimura Shoji, whose flagship was the light cruiser Naka; eight more destroyers were under the control of Rear Admiral Tanaka Raizo, plus three heavy cruisers under Rear Admiral Takagi. The Defender's ships were all built in the interim period between both world wars, with their construction being between 1920 and 1939. So, they were not in the best of repair, but most had upgraded their coms and radar to current specs, and half had removed their forward torpedo tubes among the US ships. This would play in the battle, not for the best outcomes. Also, the ships built in the interim period did not have the best watertight control doors as they did not go all the way to the top, so they were prone to flooding completely, which was adequate if you were trying to drown out a fire but could cause you to lose the ship. The USS Houston was the best armed of the flotilla, with nine 8-inch guns in three groups. Still, after her section of guns had taken a hit and could not track effectively, thus reducing her effectiveness by a third since she could not be repaired on sight and should not have been pressed into service, it was all they had to throw at the enemy. One of the main problems for this flotilla was the TBS devices because as they fired their main guns, they would knock out the TBS radios and crack their landing lights, so handheld lights were used to signal back and forth between ships. They kept hearing the Japanese floatplanes spying on them, dropping magnesium flares to let the enemy convoy know where to engage them. Does anyone know the best tactics for fighting ship to ship at night?" Andropos replied, "Sending starburst shells."

"Correct. But explain how that works to the class, please," said Major Garrison.

"First, you must have a target, then load a starburst shell and fire it along its trajectory. This will illuminate the target well enough to be seen by other guns, and they can zero in on it and hopefully destroy it," he explained.

"Excellent. But the shells fired on this case fell short and failed to backlight it. Also, the torpedoes used came from the Japanese destroyers and not a submarine, as was thought by the flotilla. This was called the Type 93 or Long Lance, and it had an even greater range than anyone thought. The firing between forces was slow for two reasons: not having a line of sight, and they had been at it for over seven hours. The Ally's ammunition was dwindling, and they had less than 50 rounds per gun available when suddenly the Japanese stopped firing. It took a minute to figure this out, and once it was realized, Doorman ordered all ships into a hard 90-degree turn to starboard because the Japanese had launched torpedoes. This tactic was used before in other engagements, and all in the battle line began their turns. This tactic called "combing," would put the torpedo into a course that would parallel the ship, thus presenting a narrower profile and attempting to mitigate any hits. This echelon turn caused all the ships to head East, but the Java would never complete her turn as word had been passed via handheld lamps from the flagship to each ship. Some had to work TBS, and others did not, so the lines of communication took a few minutes to execute, and that caused Java to be hit as her time had run out.

At 23:32, she was struck on her port bow by one of eight torpedoes launched ten minutes prior. Her aged design would show poor internal compartmentalization and an obsolete gun layout. Shortly after the explosion, a second came, and lookouts reported seeing bodies flying from the ship. There was a huge fireball, and Perth reported feeling the shockwave. Once the smoke cleared, it was determined that the second explosion came from her aft magazine, where extra ammunition was being stored. The ship began listing to one side, and there was no chance to launch the lifeboats. Most life jackets were gone in the explosion, so crew members threw anything that would float into the water and jumped in. The Perth rescued those in the water and only managed to pull 19 from the sea out of a total complement of 528. Admiral Doorman ordered the column to form around him, and they did as they were completing their final turns to go back into formation. Then, another long-lance torpedo hit the DeReyer. She lost power as her turbines were compromised. This started a fire that spread with extraordinary speed, and everything aft of the catapult was in flames. The ammunition for the Antiaircraft guns immediately began cooking off, and an oil tank had ruptured and leaked bunker fuel into and outside the ship. Because the turbines were knocked out, there was no water to fight the fire. Then the fire spread to the pyrotechnics locker, and all of it went up in a strange fireworks display. The ship was doomed. Now, what have we learned from this?"

A student said, "Always have a backup plan and an alternate rendezvous point."

"That's very good," said Major Garrison, "What else."

"Make sure that you have at least three to four different types of communication available, and all are conversant in it," said a midshipman.

"Good! What else?"

Daniel said, "Always expect the unexpected and plan for that."

They spent the next several hours analyzing the engagement, replaying all the forces' maneuvers, and determining why they did what they did and if any mistakes were made. Was it crew exhaustion? Need more information? Late information? Bad weather? Bad luck?

The following two days flew by, and he was reporting to the bay for Waterworks training. He was standing next to Major Garrison, and he informed the students. "Men, we are going into a training cycle, but remember, this bay can have navigational hazards and attack by enemy submarines. Do two things if you feel live torpedoes or Nazi U-Boats are targeting you. Squawk 'Yellow Beard' on the TBS phones and launch a flare. Then, everyone heads back to the pier with haste. We have spotter aircraft and our submarines out there. They will take care of the enemy. Any questions?"

The students were loaded up on PT boats, and each had a turn at the helm, commanding them. They were told to take them through their paces, and they raced around the harbor, shooting past buoys and crisscrossing each other's paths. They knew they were being evaluated every step of the way. The PT boats attacked a column of ships and fired dummy torpedoes. The fronts were loaded with red dye, and the tips were leather. Everyone tried getting as many hits as possible on a cruiser mockup. When they returned to the docks, they saw the rest of the PT boats were already tied up, and the crews were milling about. He tied up as well, and they disembarked.

They went around the harbor on tugboats the following day and spent time docking them and pushing barges in and out of positions. Then, after lunch, they were sent to the fireboats. When the time was called, they were all weary.

"That's all for this week." Major Garrison called, and they left the Pier talking to the evaluators. It was surreal for him. Two years into the war, he was now responsible for training men and sending them to God knows where most might be killed. It was an incredible responsibility. Major Garrison clapped him and said, "Let's get a cold one."

"Okay, but you must come to the house for dinner. I want to introduce you to my family."

"I won't turn down a home-cooked meal. But let me at least bring the beer."

"Fine by me. Let me call ahead."

They stopped, picked up some beer, and discussed the next training phase along the way.

"So, what's next for the boys?" Major Garrison asked.

"We're going to give them mark training on shallow depths in and around the river systems."

"Logical."

"Why do you ask?"

"Because I am just here to evaluate you and lend assistance. Which you don't require. You have a perfect memory and were able to give my lectures better than I could. Combat experience helps. After that, what's the next phase?"

"We will have them function as members of the crews of various ships and rotate them around. Seeing who does best at what and then submitting our evals on which ships we think they would do best on."

"See, you don't need my help anymore."

"That is a very high compliment, Major."

"What's for dinner?"

Daniel leaned out and sniffed the air as they approached the little bungalow. "Smells like Egg -Fu Young."

Enigma

Several weeks passed, and then one day, he got a call to report to Admin on the double. He was escorted into the Admiral's office, where a Coast Guard Captain was seated. The briefing began, "Mr. Core. How ready do you think your students are?"

"As ready as they will ever be."

"Excellent. Then we have a final exam for them, which will involve actual combat for them, as we have a serious problem out there."

"What is it?"

The Coastie answered, "At least one U-boat is operating in and around our coastline, and we will capture it."

"Not sink it?"

"No. Capture. Force it to the surface. We need to get their code books and their cryptography."

The Admiral said, "If we do this, we can shorten the war."

Daniel tried not to roll his eyes at this statement because hearing it after almost two years of fighting got old. Instead, he asked, "How will we execute this?"

Then, the briefing began in earnest.

The following day, he and his men reported to a warehouse at the bay, and they could all see new gun emplacements on every ship. The yard dogs had worked all night frantically to get everything ready. All mockups and simulated weapons were removed. The white flagpole they had at the front of the Patrol craft had been replaced with a one-inch gun. All weapons were now live.

A student spoke up. "Mr. Core? Is our final exam going to be a live fire exercise?" he asked.

"No. It will involve actual combat."

He could hear them murmur. "Silence in the ranks," he said.

They quieted immediately.

"This is what you have been trained for. We have a serious problem. I told you when we started that there were actual U-boats out there. Today, we will all go out and force them to the surface. We are going to capture. Not attempt to. Capture a German U-Boat. We need intelligence. We need their code books and cryptography. We are going out in a task force and will join the Coast Guard. They will be the hounds, using every tactic to drive the U-boats our way. We should meet them in Torpedo Alley. We don't know how long it will take, but be prepared to be at action stations long. Therefore, our first duty once aboard is to eat. You will eat well as it is steak and eggs. So, get to your ships and prepare to get underway at the top of the hour at zero one hundred. Good luck and good hunting!"

The men readily got to their ships, and he went to his Buckley Class Destroyer. It was powered by two Foster-Wheeler Express D water-tube boilers, two GE steam turbines that cranked out 13,500 horsepower, and two generators with 12,000 horsepower. The max speed was 24 knots, with a range of 5,500 nautical miles at about 15 knots. The bunkers could hold over 350 tons of fuel oil. At full loadout, they could displace 1,750 tons with a length of 306 feet, beam width of 36 feet, and a draft of only 11 feet. Armament of three 3-inch guns, a triple bank of 21-inch torpedoes, eight side-throwing K-gun depth charge launchers, a mark 10 Hedgehog anti-submarine mortar, and two stern depth charge racks.

It was larger than the Patrol Craft that he had been on. This was in its sea trial phase, and he was taking her through the paces. He went down to the mess deck and oversaw his men being fed. Then he retired to the officer's mess and enjoyed the steak dinner. At the appointed time, the convoy got underway, and the hunt was on in earnest.

The code name for his ship was 'Cesarian,' which in Greek was translated to 'Little Caesar.' The Coast Guard captain ship was called 'Daedalus,' the Patrol Craft was called, "Minos' and 'Apollo.' He had 50 men spread out among three boats. Both Patrol crafts had fifteen each into three eight-hour shifts. Five would take the critical command positions and rotate accordingly. If all went well, then each man would have at least an opportunity to command the Patrol Craft. But he knew that not everything would go according to plan. Once action stations were called, the men would be in their roles until the stand-down order was given.

Two hours into the patrol, Daedalus called on the TBS phone. "Cesarian. We have a contact bearing dead ahead two nautical miles from our position via hydrophone. What say you?"

"Hold one." And he called out, "Daedalus has a contact bearing two nautical miles off their position. What do you have on that heading?"

"Contact! Three Nautical Miles bearing 131.", called out the sonar operator.

"Three Nautical miles bearing 131, aye.", Daniel called out.

Daedalus called for all remaining ships in the convoy to triangulate their positions relative to sonar contact.

Daniel called the order out. "All hands put on a battle dress."

The men went to their action stations and donned protective gear of helmets and flack vests. They had been trained to make it in under thirty seconds.

Daniels's next order was, "Come right to course zero five four."

The helmsman repeated, "Coming right to course zero five four."

Daniel continued giving orders, "Engines ahead full."

"Aye, sir, engines ahead full."

Caesarians had all of the latest gear. They had a surface search radar, sonar, and a High-Frequency radio direction finder nicknamed "Huff/Duff." All of which were now in the Combat Information Center or 'CIC.' The men would use all the technology to plot the contact bearing and range. They plan it over time and could come up with an approximation of the course and speed of the contact. The Huff/Duff equipment was a tall radio antenna carried aft of the smokestacks. The receiver and scope were housed on destroyer escorts at the operator's radio shack in the aft deckhouse.

Now, they would use this technology to hunt down and try to capture at least one U-boat. But they knew their enemy hunted in packs. Therefore, they had to assume that for every contact they were aware of, there might be up to four that they were not. The good news was that this destroyer had two racks of depth charge racks on the stern, and they could roll these over the side whereby the charge housed between 300 to 600 pounds of TNT. They would sink to the set depth and then explode in the hopes that they would be within 30 yards of the enemy submarine for hull damage and 10 yards for a kill. There were also four depth charge projectors known as K guns, which would launch the depth charges on each side of the ship outwards at high angles to prevent accidental impact against the hull. This ship also carried the 24-round Hedgehog mortar rounds, which were instrumental in submarine warfare for several reasons. One is that they could be launched in an elliptical pattern forward of the ship and would only explode if the warheads hit something metallic. This mortar round was hard for the enemy subs to dodge in time as they sank quickly. The second benefit was that a competent crew could reload them in at least three minutes.

"Sound off," called Daedalus.

"Minos here. No contact."

"Apollo, spotty contact bearing 126. Range two miles."

"Cesarean, contact bearing 136. Range 1.5 miles."

"Daedalus, contact bearing 171. Range 1 mile.

"Zoey calling, dropping magnesium flare."

"Roger Zoey. Thanks for the assistance."

Zoey was the code name for a PBY Catalina twin-engine high-wing maritime patrol bomber spotter aircraft. It was called a flying boat.

A spotter called, "Left engine zero, zero five."

A second spotter called "Beacon Zero eight three."

Daniel repeated, "Beacon zero eight three."

The CIC called out, "Distance 4500."

"Fire hedgehogs!"

"Fining hedgehogs. Fining, firing, firing., called out the gunnery officer.

There was a roar as twenty-four mortars shot ahead of the ship in an elliptical arc and splashed into the sea.

"Reload!" called Daniel.

"Reloading, aye, sir," called the gunnery officer.

"Range to target and reciprocal to other vessels?"

"Range to target 4000.", called CIC, "Reciprocal 1/2 nautical mile."

"We are too far away; all engines back by 1/3."

"All engines back by 1/3, aye."

Daedalus called out, "Cesarean, keep up the pounding. We are closing the gap."

Daniel ordered, "Fire K guns depth 50 yards."

"Fining K-guns, depth 50 yards.", called the officer as the depth charges were launched to the left and right of the vessel. They careened high into the air and splashed into the water, sinking rapidly. After a few seconds, their explosive charges went off, sending geysers of water fifty feet into the air.

"Roll three starboard and two aft depth 75 yards and 30 yards respectively."

"Aye, sir. Setting charges now.", came the aft gunnery officer's response."

Twenty seconds later, the call came, "Rolling three starboard and two aft."

"Daedalus on action station.", came the call over the TBS phone.

"Firing hedgehogs."

In Daniels's mind, he pictured each ship bracketing each sub from a different direction. It was pitch black on the ocean since it was dark and there was a new moon. They didn't have the stars for illumination—just the magnesium flare, which had burned itself out already.

"Minos on station and firing hedgehogs."

"Apollo on station firing hedgehogs."

The roar was like a freight train as they expended ammunition.

"LIGHTS!" called Daedalus.

Every ship turned on its searchlights and began looking in earnest. Zoey called from overhead," We've struck oil!" which meant that the submarine had been hit by at least one of the depth charges or mortars. The sun was beginning to peek over the horizon when Daniel saw the U-Boat porpoise straight up, breaking the waves and slamming down. He could see that her bow plane was damaged. He also noticed that Daedalus was heading for her at full steam. He called out over the TBS phone, "Daedalus, you are 500 yards from rolling over the sub."

"Hard leeward! Collision alarm!"

The alarm whooped out, and there was a massive clanging of bells as the vessels activated their notices.

"Daedalus called out, "Just going to clip her. Three degrees.."

There was a thunderous crash as the vessel slammed into the submarine.

Daniel said," Ensign Reece, I need the boarding party launched aft."

"Aye, sir.", called the Ensign as he signaled Gunny Wildman to launch from the Captain's gig.

"Boarding party away!" called a watchstander.

Daniel could also see several boats launched from their respective ships, all fully armed and ready. The hatch opened up on the sub, and men started boiling out. They were screaming and choking. He could see a greenish-yellow gas escaping from other hatches. So, he called out over the loudspeakers. "GAS! GAS! All boarding parties do not shoot! Repeat, do not shoot! They are blinded. Don gas masks!"

He turned to his XO and said, "Coordinate with medical to have trauma teams standing by to receive gas casualties."

"Aye, sir," the XO said as he relayed the order.

Meanwhile, Daniel could see several Kriegsmarine dropping over the side and into the water, choking and filling their mouths with seawater to neutralize the gas's effects.

He saw two boarding parties don gas masks and dive into the forward and aft hatches to capture the code books and cryptography and prevent scuttling charges or sea valves from being opened. Opening the sea valves is a challenging process, especially when damaged. These valves allow water to enter the ship at a certain point to flood compartments and create potable drinking water. These openings shunt water into the central system used for firefighting. Each valve would have to be opened manually, so each locking screw would have to be wrenched open, and then shift a lever to keep the butterfly valve open. This would allow the flooding of the entire ship. Also, scuttling charges could be set around the coffer dams and propellers to blow and sink the boat in seconds.

Looking through his field glasses, Daniel saw a lone figure emerge from the aft hatch with a black canvas bag on his shoulder; he jumped into a waiting boat and ripped his gas mask off, triumphantly holding the bag above his head. The ship swayed away at a high rate of speed. He could also see the other boats reaching the water and retrieving the Kriegsmarine. They didn't fight as they were too severely wounded by the gas when their batteries ruptured and mixed with seawater. He saw more boarding parties exit quickly and dive overboard into the waiting boats. Just as the sun popped up and bathed the sea in an amber glow, the submarine released a "CRUMP!" sound and cracked in two. Fuel oil and debris were everywhere as she sank into the ocean's depths. He heard Daedalus call over the intercom," All small boats return to stations. Medical stand by to receive casualties."

"XO, you have the bridge!" Daniel said as he dashed to the loading area for the Captain's gig.

"XO has the bridge. AYE!"

He arrived, and the gig was raised. He could see two Kriegsmarine captives coughing badly and huddled together, obviously in full compliance as prisoners. Gunny Wildman was helping his men disembark, but Daniel could tell he was injured. "Medic!" he shouted, and they were right behind him, grabbing patients, loading them onto stretchers, and bearing them away.

"Gunny! Get yourself medical!" he ordered.

"I'm fine, skipper. Just a scratch."

"NOW!"

"Rodger that," he replied weakly.

Daniel smiled at him and said, "You are a Wildman."

The intercom went off, and the XO said, "Captain to the bridge."

Daniel reached for a TBS phone and replied, "On my way!"

When he arrived, the XO yelled, "Captain on the bridge!"

"Captain has the bridge," Daniel replied.

"I stand relieved," said the XO.

"Orders from the Admiral we are to repair back to base under radio silence. All command crews are to report to Admin, but all remaining crew members are restricted to their ships."

"Aye. Is the course laid in?"

"Aye, sir. The course is laid in."

"Ensign Marks, you have the bridge. XO, follow me to the wardroom.", said Daniel. "Yeoman Gibson has Seaman Apprentice Tom Leitzel report to the wardroom and Gunny Wildman."

The XO gave him a quizzical look, but Daniel shook his head. They went down a corridor until they reached the wardroom. He entered and switched on the radio. Then he turned and said to the XO, "I want to know what is on those recovered documents."

"Okay."

"Gunny Wildman recovered them but didn't speak German. Leitzel does. Have a Yeoman report, as we need to get an after-action report together anyway."

Wildman showed up and started, " Well, skipper, we went over as you said, and just as we reached the U-boat, Kriegsmarine started bubbling out of every orifice, but we could see that they were combat ineffective as the gas blinded them, and were busy throwing up. So, we muscled our way past them and earnestly started the boarding action. I sent three boys to the forward torpedo tubes and tried to belay any scuttling charges. But those Krauts bastards started putting up a fight. We had to put them down hard—no time for niceties like surrender. We found the head radio officer slumped over a typewriter and tools. It looked like he was trying to hack it to pieces, but it was built so well that he barely scratched it. Man, it was hot with smoke and gas everywhere, and I could feel the filter losing effectiveness. So, I had Pierce grab what he could and told him to get out with the books and typewriter. I stayed behind to grab as much residue as I could. I did not know what was valuable or not. Then we hightailed it out of there. Just in time, too, as she went up shortly after that. They couldn't let us take the win. I guess I admire them for that!"

"Sounds good. You got all that, Yeoman?" Daniel asked.

The Yeoman switched the recorder off and said. "Yes, sir. Transcribing now."

He turned as he could feel someone hovering nearby. He motioned to the shadow, looking in the doorway. "Come."

A nervous-looking teenager with hair so blonde it was white like cotton was dressed in a chambray shirt, jeans, and a white cover that he held in his hand respectfully. He gulped and asked, "You sent for me, sir?"

"Yes, I did."

"Am I in trouble?"

"Nothing of the sort. I need your help. Leitzel is a German name, right?"

"Yes, sir."

"Great."

"Can you speak, read, and write German?"

"Yes, sir."

"Good. I need these journals scanned for intelligence and translated as fast as possible. Can you do that?"

"Yes, sir."

"Excellent, they have a seat." Daniel motioned for him to sit, and he was handed a legal pad and a pencil and then given a stack of papers and notebooks of various sizes and conditions.

Leitzel looked at the various trove of treasure and quickly made two piles.

"What's that pile for?" asked the XO.

"Well, you said you needed intelligence. Given the time constraints, I doubt the cook's recipe book and the mechanic's hourly diesel expenditures cuts."

"Good plan," replied the XO.

After an hour, Leitzel looked up to the expectant faces.

"Well?" asked Daniel.

"Sir, they've been shadowing us for quite a while and even sent certain personnel to our shores in small rubber boats. These boys that went spoke perfect English with no hint of an accent."

"How is that possible?" asked the XO.

"It's called Heim ins Reich, which means back home to Germany. It was a policy issued by Adolph Hitler, convincing all Volksdeutche (ethnic Germans) living outside Nazi Germany to return home. Many did in 1938, and since they were raised here, they spoke English fluently."

"Is that in the journal?"

"No, sir."

"Then where did you find that out?"

"In a letter sent to our house by the German government."

"What else do you have?" asked Daniel.

"The first officers' log details many things about how they got into and out of the bay. Mostly they were coming in between the screws of large cargo ships."

"Gutsy!" remarked Daniel. "Anything else actionable?"

"No, sir. Just missives and laundry details; some letters to sweethearts faded from too much reading. The usual. I guess the good stuff ended up on Daedalus."

"True enough. Thanks for your help. You are dismissed from all duties; get some chow. Shower and then hit the rack. Once we get back to port, you and any other German speaker will be transferred directly to Admin to help in the line-by-line translation of all documents. No matter how mundane."

"Aye, sir," said Leitzel as he turned and left the wardroom with a bounce in his step. He was very proud to be a part of this endeavor. Half a day later, their ships were tied up at the docks, and the command crews were whisked away in cars to Admin. They were escorted into a large briefing room where what appeared to be a typewriter and some German documents and code books were lying on a table.

The Admiral said, "Gentlemen! I congratulate you on a job well done. It's a shame we could not capture the ship, but we got the most important things we wanted. I will read you in since you risked your lives for it. But you can tell no one! Your crews have received instructions not to talk about these events for less than 20 years and are all signing non-disclosure agreements.

What you see before you are an enigma machine. This is the German Cryptographic machine that we were after. It has three rotors and can provide millions of computations for coding. In their ultimate paranoia, the Kriegsmarine had instructed their operators to install a fourth rotor because they thought we were reading their mail. And they were correct because we were. We have been for some time, so this coup will be a boon for us. This training cycle is over, and your men all pass with flying colors. Be proud."

He left Admin and returned to the docks. He saw the army of lawyers set up shop in the adjacent warehouse. His men were milling around, waiting for further orders. He went to the podium and announced.

"May I have your attention?"

All talking ceased.

"I've just come from Admin, and the Admiral is very pleased with your actions. You have all passed your final exam with flying colors. I must remind you that you cannot speak of this to anyone for under twenty years unless otherwise instructed by the military. Congratulations. Return to quarters, and your ceremony will be held tomorrow at 1200 hours.

The next day, they passed in review before the Admiral and his staff. Then, there were the certificates issued and the obligatory speeches about courage and perseverance in the face of the enemy.

Quite the shindig was put on that night at the Officer's Club. He had organized to have a local Filipino Hog Farmer kill and roast his largest one. It was split down the middle and served with all of the trimmings. They even stuck an apple in its mouth. Daniel went to the party but had his family sit this out as these were all bachelors, and he just wanted to commune with the men he would be sending out to war. He hoped and prayed that he had them trained well enough. He knew that he had given them every ounce of experience that he had acquired since 1939. He needed to stop brooding and get on with it. So, he stood up and made an announcement. "GENTLEMEN! You are all about to embark on the greatest adventure known to man. In its infinite wisdom, the government has chosen you to fill the slots in the various types of ships available. I should know as I served on a Destroyer as a rating, a Minesweeper as XO in this type of training cadre, and a Patrol Craft, lastly. Not counting the shakedown cruise I was just on. Remember your training and trust in your ships and crews, as they will give all for you, and you must remember to give all back."

Sumire

Daniel was in Admin the following week, receiving orders and a blue pamphlet, and told him to report to the train station. So, he hopped into a Jeep and was told he had to sign for a package. He looked down at the pamphlet and saw a white seal and a red string binding it. He shrugged and figured it was specialized equipment or some such gear. He parked the Jeep, went to the platform, and found the mail pickup window. The postal worker looked very bored until he saw the blue pamphlet. He brightened up, looked to the side, and said, "He's here." Before Daniel got to the counter, he came out the door with a stack of paperwork. Sir? Could you please sign here and here? Then, one more. These are your copies, and now the court order is final. Here is your daughter! So sorry it took us so long to get her to you.", he said as he reached into the door and gently pulled a young Japanese girl out into the hallway. She wore a plain brown dress with scuffed Mary Janes and Bobby Socks. Her eyes were shining, and she bowed deeply. Then ran into his arms, crying, "Daddy!"

He had to cover his shock and surprise. "Sorry, Sumire. I did what I could as fast as I could."

She spun him about, grabbed her case off the bench, and said calmly, conspiratorial, "Let's just get out of here."

They exited the platform and drove away, with the watchful eyes of the Postal Clerk waving them goodbye. He went a block and a half, then pulled over and stopped the Jeep. He looked down at the paperwork, a court order by a Judge awarding him and his wife sole custody of one Sumire Subbaya, now Sumire Core.

"I'm sorry to be such trouble, Mr. Core.", she said as she saw the wheels turning in his head.

"You're no trouble. I asked to get you out of there, and this is the solution."

"But I'm not your daughter."

"You are now."

She made to get out of the Jeep, and he stopped her. "What do you think you are doing, young lady?"

"Getting out."

"Why?"

"Because I'm not your responsibility."

"Yes, you are. You have been since I married my wife. She made your grandparents the godparents of her children with reciprocity. So, since they have both died, you are now my daughter. Full stop. You are my responsibility until the day I die. You are my family, no matter what!" he said as tears came down his cheeks.

She looked into his eyes and saw that he would take a bullet for her; she surged forward into his arms and cried. They both called for a few minutes until a light was tapping on the windshield from a Police Officer.

"What seems to be the holdup?" he asked quizzically.

"Sorry, Officer, I just picked up my daughter from the train station and got emotional, so I had to pull over."

"Haven't seen her in a while since the war started?"

"You could say that."

"Move along!" he said, swinging his nightstick to the right.

"Roger that!" Daniel said as he put the Jeep into drive and hightailed it back to the base. He went straight to admin, got her fingerprinted, added her to the roster, and obtained her ID card. Then they drove home.

He pulled up and beeped the horn twice. Hailey looked out the window, and her face turned white. She burst out the door, jumped down the stairs, and hugged Sumire so hard she knocked the wind out of her.

Miranda was crying and was right behind Hailey. Sumire hugged Miranda back, and they were all blubbering. Daniel grabbed Sumire's luggage and went up the steps, taking off his shoes. Jack was looking up from the floor, reading a comic book.

"What's up, Daddy?"

"You have a new sister. Her name is Sumire. She was your neighbor on Kona."

"How did she go from being a neighbor to a sister?"

"When your mother joined the military, she had to sign paperwork stating that if anything happened to her, your guardian..."

"Guardian?"

"Yes, an adult that will care for you in the event of your parent's death or disability."

"Ok, I think I understand."

"Right, so the military required two different people to do this. Since your Auntie is your only living relative, if she died as well, your care would go to what is known as a Godparent."

"That's a strange name."

"It is, but it's necessary."

"So, what happened?"

"Sumire was living with her grandparents when the war broke out. Because we were at war with Japan, many Japanese people were taken away to live in camps."

"Why?"

"Because bad things might happen to them."

"Why?"

"Because people fear what they don't understand."

"Why?"

"I wish I knew."

"But she looks like us. Well, not you but us, us."

"She does look similar. But there are differences. If you know how to look."

"How is she different?"

"Bone structure."

"What?"

"See her face. Notice how all of you have a more rounded one, and hers is slenderer."

"Maybe."

"It's okay. You can learn it over time."

While talking, the women moved into the kitchen and talked animatedly. Sumire donned an apron and searched around for

ingredients. Miranda shot Daniel a wary look but just shrugged, mouthing, 'Let her do it.' He held his hands out in surrender.
Sumire heated a pan, chopped up some hot dogs, and started pan-frying them; then, she added sugar, soy sauce, and a little onion. She spooned the mixture into a bowl and covered the dish. Miranda shoved her aside and began to blanch the vegetables. Sumire looked at Daniel and mouthed, 'It's her kitchen.' He held his hands out in surrender a second time.
He heard the thrum of an engine and knew that his wife was home. He recognized the purring of that sports car anywhere. She came up the walkway with a spring in her step and kicked off her shoes, grabbing Daniel as she kissed him. Jack looked up and said with disgust, "Blech," as he got up and put his comic book away. He was then headed to the bathroom to wash up without being told to.
Kim-Yee was looking into Daniels's eyes with love and said, "Wow, something smells good. What's cooking?" She turned and saw the girl. She said softly, "Sumire?"
Sumire held her arms out, crying as she rushed to embrace Kim-Yee. "Oba." (Japanese for Auntie), she said. Then, she corrected herself, "Sorry, it's Okaasan now." (Japanese for mother)
Kim-Yee looked shaken. "What?"
"Yes, definitely Okaasan!" said Sumire as she turned around and went to the table, calling Hailey "Ane."(elder sister in Japanese)
Jack corrected her, "She's Gajee." (elder sister in Chinese).
Sumire said demurely. "Yes, Jack, to you, she is your Gajee. But to me, she is my Ane."
Kim-Yee was starting to swoon, and Daniel grabbed her. The reality of what was being said was beginning to hit home. They both sat on the couch hard, both with looks of shock on their faces. Kim-Yee started talking out of the side of her mouth at Daniel.
"What in the hell just happened?"
"Remember when you told me to take care of Sumire?"
"Yes."
"Well? I did, and the solution was the court awarded me her."
"How?"

"Well, when you signed that paperwork making the Subbaya's the godparents of the children."

"I remember."

"It had a reciprocity clause that you also signed."

"Go on."

"When we married, that transferred to me, and now, because they are gone, she is our daughter. Full Stop."

Kim-Yee blew out a long breath. "I need some whiskey.", she said as she got up from the couch with an air of finality. She marched over to the icebox, got the half bottle of McClelland's, and opened it, retrieving a Coke bottle. Miranda handed her three glasses, and she poured three doubles. All the adults clinked glasses together and drained the contents in one long gulp.

Then Kim-Yee smiled, turned to the children, and clapped her hands, "All right, troops, time to wash up." Both girls promptly left the table, but Jack stayed. His mother shot him a look, but he proudly held his hand out, and she could see they were still damp. He smugly declared, "And I didn't even have to be told."

She nodded and started to assemble the eating utensils. Miranda placed the vegetables on the table, and Daniel picked up the wooden bucket they used to store the cooked rice and placed it at the end of the table. Chopsticks were passed around, and once everyone was seated, the rice was added to each bowl. Then, the covers of the dishes were removed, and everyone used their chopsticks to get what they wanted. In Jack's case, he asked for what he couldn't reach, and it was placed in his bowl for him.

Kim-Yee said, "Danny, I think we need to get a lazy Susan, don't you think?"

"Sure. It would make things easier."

"What's this?" Kim-Yee asked as she tasted the new dish.

"Shoyu Weenies. I learned how to cook then in camp.", Sumire said.

"Very tasty."

"Well, we had to make do," Sumire said frankly. "And these vegetables are divine."

Miranda said, "Eat up, young one. There is plenty."

So, she did. They were amazed at how much food Sumire could put away.

Once dinner was over, the girls started washing the dishes and talking animatedly. Kim-Yee and Daniel went out on the veranda. "Danny, is this for real?"

"Yes! Here is the paperwork.", he said exasperatedly.

"I said, 'Do Something!' And this was your solution?"

"No, I only inquired about her. The paperwork was already in place. My inquiry activated it."

"What are we going to do?"

"Do? She's already on the books."

"What does that mean?"

"That she's ours. Period. They even changed her last name to match mine."

"Oh, that's just great! My children don't even have your last name."

"You mean our children?'

"Yes, sorry. I mean our children."

"How is this going to work?"

"She is listed on all paperwork as our daughter. She has a military pass and is on the books as a dependent. Full stop."

He saw her blanch a little at the sternness of his declaration but then nodded meekly. "Okay. I will honor my agreement with her grandparents and love her until my death. I swear."

They felt eyes upon them as they both turned, and the rest of the family ran towards them, and they embraced in a group hug.

Later that evening, as they sat in bed, neither one could sleep.

"How is this going to work?" Kim-Yee asked Daniel.

"We've been over this.", he said tiredly.

"No, I mean, how will she go to school? Will she be mistreated? Will she have to talk about who she is?" she asked.

"I don't know. But I think the way has already been paved, so we must see how it works. I doubt any children could tell a Japanese girl from a Chinese one, and her name matches.

"But how will we explain why she is arriving now?" Kim-Yee asked.

"Just say that she was attending a different school in Hawaii with a different school year."

"Isn't that lying?"

"No. Because it's true, let's sleep on it, and I'm sure it will all be fine in the morning. I'll sign her in as I have her school records."

The next day, after breakfast, he piled the children into the Jeep and drove them to the base school. Hailey and Jack jumped out and headed to their respective lines. He walked Sumire to the office and signed her in. He handed off the documents to the secretary, who looked down at them and motioned for him to follow her into a small office, where she shut the door. They sat, and she looked at him sternly.

"Spit it out.", he told her.

"Mr. Core," she began crisply. "We understand that your children are of Chinese descent."

"Yes, that is correct."

"But here it stated that Summer.."

"Sumire. It's pronounced Sue-Mire-ey."

"Fine, Sumire. Is Japanese."

"Yes."

"Did you lie to us?"

"No. She was my goddaughter, and upon the deaths of her grandparents, the court awarded me her and made the adoption final. You can see that in the paperwork. So now she is my daughter. What seems to be the problem?"

"Well, there are several children here whose loved ones have been killed by the Japanese."

"And there are several here who've probably lost loved ones at the hands of the Germans and Italians. What is your point?"

"Do you think this school is the best place for her now?"

"Madame, currently, we are at war. This is a World War, and everyone is fighting hard to end it. Sumire is an American. She has spent the last couple of years as a prisoner in an internment camp because she was born Japanese. She is a child. Just let her be that. I doubt any children would know a Japanese person on sight. She has Hailey, and I hope you will put them in the same classes. If you say nothing, then there won't be any problems. Anything else?"

She seemed deflated, "No."

"Great." then he walked out and up to Sumire. He handed her $5 and said, "Use this money to buy what you need for clothes and sundry items at the PX. Hailey will show you where it is. We must go into town for whatever you can't find."

He then strode out of the building and to the waiting Jeep.

Thanksgiving Day, 1943

It was a cool, crisp morning on Thursday, November 25, 1943. The women had spent the past several days cooking the assorted delicacies for a holiday, and now they piled into the War Wagon and drove out to Daniels Family Home on Ashley Phosphate Road. They pulled into the driveway a little before 9 am and began marching up the stairs with assorted pots and pans. Everyone was bearing something.

The food was stacked in the kitchen, and the women got to work. His mother, Midora, was fussing over Sumire, saying in Greek, 'You're too skinny. We've got to put some meat on those bones.' Sumire might not have understood the words, but she got the message. She just smiled and nodded meekly.

He had given her money to buy new clothing, but she was still wearing the clothes she had made from old flour and rice sacks and dyed indigo with what Hailey had mailed her. He decided to take her shopping tomorrow. The interesting thing about the flour sacks was that the company knew that people were making clothing, so they made them out of floral prints to help the customers. The labels would wash out, and everyone was happy. Plus, it was good publicity and helped the economy.

His sister Diana came and joined him in the living room.

"Hey, there, squirt."

"What happened? Did they kick you out?"

"Yep. Mom said to leave because I can burn water."

He chuckled at the thought of it. "So, what's the news from our loved ones?" he asked.

"Interesting that you should ask. Thea is, of course, working in the Women's Auxiliary Ferrying Squadron and moving planes from the factory to the staging areas for transport. She sent a journal of her exploits that you might want to read. I put all of her letters with it."

"How very thoughtful of you."

"Ristarnt also shipped a journal, but he had to bake it into a fruitcake. Since that's a big no-no, I guess he thought it was important enough,

111

or he felt that if he didn't make it through the war, his story and squadron would not be forgotten."

The day passed swiftly; the women chattered in the kitchen, and the men folk listened to the news and sporting events on the radio. The family shared a large meal and gave thanks. His mother prayed for those who weren't present, and then they said their goodbyes and went home.

Once they returned to their home on base, they started preparations for the hotpot. Hotpot was a communal meal cooked in a cast iron cauldron. It consisted of a broth and different types of vegetables cut up and arranged in the pot in a circular pattern. There were mushrooms, pieces of tofu, clear bean thread noodles, tong-ho, and other vegetables, like white and green onions. All this was placed on a charcoal brazier in the middle of the table. Then, a plate of thinly sliced meat was seated next to it, and each family member was given a bowl of rice and a smaller bowl of a whisked egg. Then, they could soak the meat in the egg and add it to the soup. They would generally let it boil for a few minutes, then scoop out what they wanted and eat it over the rice. It was a lovely communal meal in winter and on special occasions.

Jack found that dipping the meat into the egg was too cumbersome, so they just added his egg to the soup and ladled it onto his rice bowl when it was done.

Sumire enjoyed the hot pot as she had not had it for several years. He kept seeing a series of conflicting emotions cross her face and wondered what was wrong.

After the meal, they all sat around the radio to listen to the news, but it was all about the war, so they turned it off and played some records. He drifted onto the veranda, and within a few minutes, Sumire came out and said, "Chichi? (Japanese for father).

"Yes."

"Did I do something wrong?"

"No, dear. Why do you ask?"

"Because you kept staring at me during dinner."

"I was just noticing that you seemed happy but also seemed to have guilt over it. I was wondering what was causing it."

"Nothing. Everything.", she said dejectedly.

"It's an adjustment. But now you are here for good and will be well cared for."

"I know that. I can feel it. But it all just seems so unfair. I was born an American and then treated like the enemy."

"Made you feel lost and alone."

"Yes. There was so much despair in the camps. We tried everything to keep moving."

"Like what?"

"Like having a newspaper. Holding plays and variety shows. Playing baseball and basketball. Anything to keep our spirits up. Then they came for the men and said they needed help with the harvesting. They never returned. We heard they were shipped to the mainland to help with work once the harvest was over. Then, they asked for volunteers to join the Army and form an all-Nisei unit. They disappeared. One by one, every little bit of me was taken away. What if the war never ends?"

"What are you truly asking?"

"What if they come for me again?"

"Then I will fight for you."

"How?"

"Any way that I can. You are here because I had to get you out of there."

She hugged him and then turned away and went back into the house. Kim-Yee walked around the corner. "Wow! They did a number on her."

"Yes, her spirit is bruised but not broken. All we can do is show her love; hopefully, the wounds in her soul will mend."

She hugged him, and they looked at the stars, holding each other and enjoying the salubrious breezes from the bay.

The next day, he took Sumire and Hailey shopping for clothing and enjoyed spending time with his girls. Sumire seemed to be adjusting well to life on the mainland. He just hoped that her ordeal was over for now. While the girls were shopping, he sat holding the bags as they tried on the latest fashions on King Street and got to thinking. He wondered how long the war was going to last. He had joined in 1939, and after four years, he was tired of it. At that time, he served as Gunner's mate and was breveted to warrant officer. Then, it is sent through OCS and given a commission. At the end of the year, he was more than likely to be promoted up the chain. He wasn't sure if they would ever give him another ship since the last one was sunk. But it was war, and the service's needs dictated what would happen. His eye was healing, and he was busy training the next group of officers to handle liturgical ships of all shapes and sizes. The only way to win this war was with more men, officers, training, and hulls for the navy, aircraft, tanks, trucks, jeeps, and munitions for the army.

The whole world had gone mad, and the only thing that he could do was to continue to fight. He wasn't fighting for the sake of doing it for glory. He was fighting against what he felt was a great evil in the world, and if a good man does nothing, then that is evil enough. He wasn't raised to be a quitter, hated a bully, and genuinely felt that the Japanese and Germans needed to be stopped at all costs. The problem was that the butcher's bill was running high, and he was running out of steam. Maybe that was why he was put on the beach. He was grateful for the change in recharging his mental batteries. But he still felt like he wasn't doing enough. His last campaign was an 18-month stint in Alaska, ferrying troops, providing escort duties for hospital ships, and running groceries, parts, and ammo. But he kept going back and forth between Alaska and Hawaii. He thought that his life was pretty standard. Take a business trip and return home while others are pounded at it daily.

He was reading the letters, journals, and dairies of his family members, friends, and colleagues. He was starting to group them into proper order and was going to chronicle them because he didn't want their sacrifices to go unremembered in history. Everyone was doing their part, and he supposed this was his. To let their stories be told. He wasn't much of a storyteller, but he felt it was his duty now to give them their spot in history. The winners write history, and he aimed to be on the winning team. He just hoped that it would end soon because war is terrible. He remembered a quote from history class in school from Robert E. Lee: "It is well that war is so terrible. Otherwise, we should grow too fond of it."

Then there was the quote from his Union counterpart William Tecumseh Sherman, " I am tired and sick of war. Its glory is all moonshine. It is only those who have neither fired a shot nor heard the shrieks and groans of the wounded who cry aloud for blood, for vengeance, for desolation. War is hell."

As he pondered these quotes, he saw the girls stride forward with more purchases and smiled. Knowing that all he had done was for their benefit, he fought for them and all mankind. He felt that he could live with that or die trying. He had come close to death several times. Too close as far as he was concerned. But he never feared for himself. He only feared for those he might end up leaving behind.

If you enjoyed reading this book, please go online and provide an honest review. Amazon.com: Shining Through: Battles in the Pacific: 9781958297278: Corzo, Donovan D: Books

Bibliography:
Military Nursing World War II — American Nursing History
http://womenofwwii.com/navy-nurses/
History of American Nurses World War II (squarespace.com)
Grace Under Fire: The Army Nurses of Pearl Harbor, 1941 - PubMed
(nih.gov)

Preview of Book 4

Up in The Clouds

Dear Brothers,

Everyone is doing their part for the war effort, and now the wild child is at it again. She was seeing that boy Lee Skipper, who had always been a bit rowdy. Well, his uncle Dave has a crop-dusting plane, and Lee took T up in it one night, and she was hooked. Lee had always treated her well and didn't mind when I tagged along with her a time or two. Anyway, she joined up with the coastal watchers, and when an opening came up for the Civil Air Patrol, she immediately went down and signed up. Now, she goes out most days screaming around the skies. I don't think she ever wants to land that thing.

In other news, there are a lot of soldiers, sailors, and airmen in the area for coastal defense. This means that the USO throws a lot of dances and parties. Momma makes us go to them, but I don't like it. Officers were pawing at me. I prefer to see the real men and dance with them as they are in the thick of it, and they are always respectful and grateful, whereas the officers treat us as objects. The curfews and blackouts are depressing, but we are at war and can't be helped. Know that I pray for every one of you every day. I want you all to return home safe and sound. I know that might not be possible, but I can sleep safely knowing you all are doing your duty.

Your loving sister,

Diana

Daniel smiled at that. It was Thanksgiving Day, 1943, and the country had been at war for over two years. All the able-bodied men and women of his family had joined up. He had joined in 1939 when he witnessed German U-boats sinking ships from a convoy headed to Britain that had launched from Charleston, SC. He even had a Captain ticket, as his grandfather had been a tugboat captain and wanted to leave the business to a family member, and he seemed to be the only one interested. So, he had worked tirelessly for a year to earn that Captain's Certificate, and then the world went crazy. After witnessing the destruction of the ships, he went home, and when he walked in, his grandfather just knew. He didn't have to say anything. Grandad just got up and began packing a seabag, handing it to him.

"If a good man does nothing, then that is evil enough. Go forth and help conquer that evil. But remember, you will only be a wheel in a cog. They will tell you your place. Please don't fight with them or argue because cream rises, no matter what. Your time will come."

They had got in the truck, and he went to the induction site. He disembarked, never looking back.

The Navy had sent him to basic, then on to gunnery school. He made it to the rate of second class and was pretty good at what he did but always struggled with math. They wouldn't even consider him for a Warrant Officer, which he felt was unfair, but then he remembered his grandfather's wisdom and just shrugged it off. Then, his ship was attacked in the Coral Sea, and all the officers were killed. Before he died, Mr. Begley pinned the rank of Warrant Officer to his collar. He had acting Captaincy and was told to "FIGHT THE SHIP." The Captain had left a battlefield promotion in his safe for this eventuality. Daniel fought off the enemy, the elements, the fires, and the sea. He got the ship and crew to safety and was escorted to the Commodore, who took his statement and sent him off to Pearl Harbor to see Admiral Nimitz, who was impressed and set him up at Officers Candidacy School.

While waiting for his slot to open, he met Kim-Yee, and the two had a whirlwind romance. He graduated and was commissioned as a Lieutenant Junior Grade. This allowed him to skip the rank of Ensign. Kim-Yee had been at the ceremony in San Francisco and had even hitched a ride with Nimitz to be there. She had dropped the bombshell of their fifteen-year age difference and that she had two children from a previous marriage. He didn't care. He proposed to her, and they married immediately. Now, looking back, he couldn't imagine a life without them.

***

Dearest brothers,

I know you are all at war and doing all you can to end it. So am I. My job is to deliver the materials so you may continue fighting. It's not glamorous. But there is danger. We've lost some girls through training accidents and bad weather. I will write as often as I can.

Your loving sister

Thea

Daniel looked down at the correspondence that his sister had sent home. This was going to take a while. He needed to organize her letters and coordinate them with her diary entries. She had sent them back for a reason. He knew that there was an inherent danger in what she was doing. She might not be dodging bullets and enemy aircraft, but she could still be killed through lousy weather, nonworking instruments, or mechanical failure. She was just one pilot, yet she had to fly every available craft. That took a lot of training and a certain amount of Moxie, which Thea had in spades.

He remembered when they were growing up, Thea never really liked to wear dresses. She was a Tomboy at heart, always stealing his spare clothing. Several times, she was mistaken for a boy and just went along with it since she had a bit of an androgynous build. His mother was constantly nagging her about not being very ladylike, and she threatened to tear off all her clothes and run around naked. She was pretty spirited at the age of ten. Now, she was continuing on the same type of path. Always trying to prove that whatever a male could do, she could do, and sometimes even better. He and his brothers always had to keep an eye on her since she was a bit of a trouble magnet. She never did anything maliciously. She just attracted trouble like lightning. Since it was a holiday, he wondered if he could reach her. He got up from his leather chair in his office and called the base operator.

"Operator, I need a long-distance line to Harlow Field in Texas."

"Is this a military call or private?"

"It's a personal call from Daniel Core to his sister Thea."

119

"I'll try, sir, but because of the holiday, it might take longer. Please stay by the phone for the next hour."

"Thanks, and Happy Thanksgiving." he hung up the phone and sat back, thinking. He made a mental note to ask his wife, Kim-Yee, to make a plate of sandwiches and send them to the girls at the switchboard.

Just then, the phone rang, and he picked it up.

The operator spoke, "Lt. Core, I have the long-distance line to Harlow Field."

"Thanks"

"Connecting you."

"Thea?"

"Yes, Darian. Happy Thanksgiving."

"How have you been?"

"Busy."

Doing what?"

"Keeping my skills up in the clouds."

"What are you flying these days?"

BT-17 trainers. I've been ferrying them from the factories to wherever they are needed. How's the family? I heard we have a new edition."

"Yes. I've got another daughter. She's around Hailey's age."

"Did you have a girl on the side?"

"No. She's my goddaughter and a war orphan."

He heard the line click twice, warning him that he had only seconds left before they had to clear the bar for military traffic.

"I heard it too," Thea said dejectedly.

"I love you and can't wait to fill you in on everything. I'm stationed at home. For now. Gotta go."

"Bye"

Then the line went dead.

He laid the phone in the cradle and went into the kitchen. He saw his three children all sprawled on the couch, snoring away. Hailey was the spitting image of her mother and thirteen: Sumire, his twelve-year-old Japanese daughter, and Jack, his five-year-old son. Hailey and Jack were his wife's children from a previous marriage, but they were his children to them. Kim-Yee smiled at him and nodded to her elder sister Miranda, who had her feet up in his comfy leather chair, with a washcloth covering her eyes. Everyone was worn out from the festivities of Thanksgiving. They had all overeaten and were napping as a result.

He grabbed some slices of bread and started putting together a sandwich. She scolded him," You can't be hungry still."

"Oh no. These are for the girls that work the switchboard."

"What?"

"They got me a long-distance call to Thea, so I thought I would surprise them with a plate."

"Good thinking. Let's make one upright."

About five minutes later, they had assembled a decent-sized platter and wrapped it in tin foil. He went to the Jeep he had signed from the motor pool and drove the two blocks to the communications shack. The weather was grey and overcast. Typical for Charleston, South Carolina. He parked and walked to the door. He opened it and strode in.

It was a typical office set up with a receiving counter. There was a very stern-looking matron type who looked up as he walked in. She said in a very crisp tone, "Lieutenant."

"Hey there. I just wanted to cheer you up since you have to work on a holiday."

Her face brightened up. "Girls. Come up here."

He could see behind her was a bay of switchboards that could easily accommodate twenty, ten on each side. But there were only four on duty.

They all unplugged their headsets and came up to the front.

The matron hit a switch, which transferred the calls to her headset.

"Look at what this nice young officer has brought us," she said as she opened the tin foil to reveal turkey sandwiches.

They all brightened, and there were a couple of squeals of excitement.

"I just wanted to thank you all for letting me talk to my sister. Even though it was only for a minute or two, it was priceless."

He smiled as they dove in and waved goodbye as he returned to the Jeep.

He drove home and walked up the stairs to his little bungalow. He was removing his shoes at the threshold. He went to his office and picked up the correspondence. He found a letter she had sent him when she first signed up.

Vmail: Hey brother,

I've gone and done it. I've signed up for the Civil Air Patrol. It took a while to get myself certified as we had to pay a portion of our fuel for training. The hardest part was the dead reckoning we needed to perform to show proficiency. And since I worked at the factory for a while, I had saved enough money to pay the fees. But now I have my pilot's license. I heard about the women's ferrying position for aircraft so that I will look into it.

All my love,

Thea

He put that letter to the side and looked at the next one. This time, it was a letter from his twin brother Thanos.

www.ingramcontent.com/pod-product-compliance
Lightning Source LLC
Chambersburg PA
CBHW061252170626
46809CB00007B/2957